Songs of Innocence

Songs of Innocence

A Hannah Weybridge thriller

Anne Coates

Urbane
PUBLICATIONS

urbanepublications.com

First published in Great Britain in 2018 by Urbane Publications Ltd
Suite 3, Brown Europe House, 33/34 Gleaming Wood Drive, Chatham, Kent ME5 8RZ
Copyright © Anne Coates, 2018

A CIP catalogue record for this book is available from the British Library.

ISBN 978-1-911331-54-4
MOBI 978-1-911331-56-8

Design and Typeset by Julie Martin
Cover by Julie Martin

Printed and bound by 4edge UK

Urbane
PUBLICATIONS

urbanepublications.com

For Olivia and Harriet

Can I see another's woe,
And not be in sorrow too?
Can I see another's grief,
And not seek for kind relief?

William Blake, *On Another's Sorrow*

CHAPTER ONE
Peckham Rye, London May 1994

Early morning in Peckham Rye Park composed its own symphony. An excited bark from an unseen dog. Birds sounding out their morning chorus high in the trees. A rustle of branches and leaves as a squirrel bounded from one tree to the next. The caw of a crow. A fox scratching the ground before marking the territory with his scent.

Two young boys sneaked around the lake – known locally as the Pond – to the far side and leapt over the low fence which bore the sign: No Fishing. No Bathing. Both were wearing dark hoodies, jeans and trainers that were cheap and without a fashionable logo. The smaller of the two slipped and landed awkwardly near the water's edge.

"Shit." A few stones he had disturbed splashed into the lake.

"Shh," said the other looking around, but only the ducks and Canada geese had heard and they showed a marked disinterest.

"How deep d'you think it is, Ollie?"

The other boy shrugged. "Dunno." He elbowed his friend in the ribs. "Deep enough to cover you, Jace."

Jason eyed the murky water with suspicion and shuffled backwards on his bottom. The boys unpacked their rucksacks in companionable silence.

Quickly they assembled their fishing tackle. Ollie opened the tin of bait and grinned as he took a moment to select a worm and handed the tin to his freckle-faced friend. They sat on the bank, partially hidden by a clump of bushes tall enough to make them less conspicuous. A large rat ran along the water's edge near the reeds. Jason shuddered. He hated rats ever since he'd seen one eating rotting leftover food from a split black rubbish bag in the stairwell in their block of flats.

"Ready?"

"Ready."

Together they cast their lines. The plop of their baited hooks caused a slight ripple, which ruffled a moorhen's feathers as it glided past. A mandarin duck with its spectacular red, orange, white and blue plumage perching on a low branch just skimming the water, raised its head but showed no curiosity in the boys.

Peace prevailed. Jason felt his eyelids grow heavy, his long lashes brushing his cheeks. Ollie nudged him. "Don't fall asleep, wanker."

"I'm not." Jason wiped his sleeve across his nose and sniffed.

Ollie handed him a sandwich from a sliced loaf bag he'd had in his rucksack and munched on one himself. Chocolate spread. His favourite. "I love it here. It's like the country where my nan lives."

Jason nodded though he'd never been anywhere really. Never somewhere as exotic and exciting as he imagined the country to be. His whole world was the council estate where he lived with his mum on the seventeenth floor of their tower block, and school. Both were intimidating and harsh. He only ever came to the park when Ollie invited him.

"Where does your nan live then?"

"Harlow. There's a field and a brook at the bottom of her garden. I love it there. Love it." Ollie finished his sandwich and threw the crusts to the pigeons patiently waiting nearby.

Suddenly Jason's line tightened. "I think I've got something."

Ollie helped him reel in. A small fish neither could identify wriggled on the hook. Both boys were too excited to notice that they had also disturbed something else that floated to the surface. A coot rose in a flurry of wings and seemed to scream out at the boys who looked up from their task to see a face staring out of the water. Then a hand emerged and appeared to point directly at them as the terrified fishermen both let out an almighty yell.

Jason and Ollie were sitting a few inches apart at the back of the park-keeper's van, their legs dangling above the ground. The groundsman had been alerted, along with the police, by a man and a woman walking their dogs on the other side of the Pond. They had heard the boys' screams and raced over, moving them away from their grim discovery. The woman and her dog went off to make the necessary phone call. The ashen-faced man was now sitting on a bench idly stroking his dog's head, placed in sympathy, on his lap. His trousers were wet from the knees down, having dragged the body from the Pond. Just in case... but there was no doubt. The girl was dead.

No one said a word as DS Mike Benton approached. The boys looked so young and vulnerable, he thought, but the little blighters had been fishing illegally. Sergeant Benton shook the smile from his face. He recognised his younger self in them. He'd been brought up in a similar area of south London and hadn't been averse to breaking the rules. But fortunately he'd never discovered a dead body as they had. That had come later. Much later.

Uniform had done a thorough job of sealing off the area and most of the regulars who walked their dogs just gave the lake a cursory glance and carried on, eager to keep their distance and maintain the momentum of their morning. Only a few stood around to see what the action was about.

In an attempt to be less intimidating, DS Benton crouched down by the van so that the boys were looking down at him. The younger boy was sniffing. His freckles stood out in marked contrast to the paleness of his skin. The other boy's red-rimmed eyes belied his nonchalant air.

"So, Jason, Ollie –" he'd been given their names by uniform – "I think we'd better get you home, don't you?"

Jason wiped his hand across his face. "Me mum's goin' t' kill me."

Ollie shot him a look, which clearly told him to shut up.

"Don't worry, you won't be in any trouble." Benton smiled in what he hoped was a reassuring manner.

The boys' faces betrayed their suspicion of all adults, especially the police. Distrust of anyone in authority was part and parcel of growing up on their estate.

"It's been a terrible shock for you, I know." He paused

trying to find the right words. "But you've probably saved another family a lot of heartache. They will be able to grieve for their daughter and not keep wondering where she is."

The boys nodded not knowing what the hell the detective was on about.

"D'you know who she is?" Ollie asked.

"Not yet, son, not yet. But we will – soon enough."

"Is the Pond very deep?" Jason shuddered remembering how he had nearly slipped in.

"Deep enough." He signalled to two women who were waiting nearby. "These ladies will take you home and explain to your parents that you're not in any trouble but that we will need to take a statement from you at the station. Okay?" The boys nodded again and slid down from the van. "Just one thing." The boys looked at him, expecting the worst. "No more fishing in the lake, okay?"

"Yes sir," they chorused.

"And if you want to talk about anything they'll give your parents a number to call." Benton watched them go, guessing that any thought of fishing, with or without permission, would be far from their minds for a long time to come. He strolled over to have a word with the man sitting on the bench.

In contrast to the grim discovery in the lake, sunlight flickered through the treetops with a tantalising promise of a warm afternoon to come. Benton had stood by the body while the photographer moved around taking shots from every angle. A beautiful face slightly bloated from its time in the water, with a fine line of white foam around the mouth.

What the hell was so bad that she had to do this? He wasn't usually given to introspection but the sight of the dead girl moved him. Some poor parents were going to have their hearts broken today. He hoped he wouldn't have to be the one who broke the news to them, whoever they were. But he knew that more than likely the task would fall to him. And it never got any easier.

There wasn't much left to do. Thrusting his hands in his pockets, he looked across the lake where he spotted a familiar figure pushing a buggy and made his way over to her.

"Well, well, Ms Hannah Weybridge. To what do we owe the pleasure of your illustrious presence here? A Peckham drowning's hardly national news, is it?"

"Nice to see you too, Sergeant." Hannah glared at the man who had given her such a hard time when she'd found Liz Rayman's body only a few months previously. He'd gone out of his way to be rude and nasty as she had tried to make sense of her friend's murder. His boss, DI Claudia Turner, even had to reprimand him on a couple of occasions. But she never made excuses for him. She didn't allow personal issues to impinge on her professionalism and didn't expect it from her team either as both Hannah and the sergeant had learned.

However Hannah, when she'd swallowed her irritation at this man's interruption of her stroll with her daughter, noticed a marked change in Mike Benton. He looked younger, in fact. His hair had been cut and styled. His clothes looked fresh and fitted him better. And those laughter lines around his eyes that she'd noticed before seemed as though they were more often in use.

"You're looking well. A lot better than the last time I saw you."

Benton scanned the sky, shading his eyes with a hand. "Things change. Improve." He stared across the lake. "But not for that young lady. Looks like she topped herself."

His casual dismissal of a life angered Hannah but she'd learned not to let her emotions show. Especially not to the likes of Benton. She glanced over at the tent, which had been erected on the far side. She'd been surprised when she saw all the police cars in the parking area. A walk in the spring sunshine with Elizabeth was a rare treat. One she didn't want hijacked.

The toddler was struggling to get out of the buggy. "Ducks," she shouted, then turned to Benton to give him the full force of her smile. "Elizabeth feed the ducks."

To Hannah's surprise he knelt beside the buggy. "Not today, sweetheart." Elizabeth looked mutinous. "But you can still go to the swings over there." He pointed to the play area.

Elizabeth considered this for a moment then turned to her mother with a happier expression. "Swings, Mama."

Hannah was grateful for the distraction. "Well I'll leave you to it, Sergeant. I'm not here in a professional capacity as you can see. I daresay the local press will be demanding your attention."

She turned the buggy towards the playground. "I'm glad things are going better for you." And she meant it. But she couldn't help wondering about the body they'd found in the lake. Usually the park-keeper's biggest concern was the terrapins who'd colonised the Pond after being dumped there by owners who'd grown tired of them.

By the time she'd reached the playground, with Elizabeth now trotting beside her and stopping every few minutes to inspect any stone, insect or blade of grass that caught her attention, Hannah had managed to put aside all thoughts about the body in the lake. Although she did speculate about what had caused DS Benton's transformation.

Playing on the swings and slides had Elizabeth shrieking in delight, especially when she found a little playmate who chased her round and played hide and seek in the Wendy house. Hannah smiled at the other mother who, she guessed, was at least ten years her junior. She returned the smile but looked bored and moved away to sit on a swing, rarely looking at her son as he raced around. Hannah was happy to see Elizabeth enjoying his company. She let her thoughts drift back to the Pond and DS Benton but didn't take her eyes off her daughter. Some twenty minutes later, Elizabeth was coaxed out of the play area and into her buggy where she promptly fell into a contented doze.

Hannah envied her. Sleep was something that didn't come to her easily now. Every sound was a potential threat, every shadow a menace. But this afternoon the shadows cast by the spring sunshine were soothing as she ambled through the Japanese garden then on to the Rye, making her way home.

The last thing she expected to see as she turned into

her road was a police car parked outside her house and, standing by her gate speaking into her mobile phone, DI Claudia Turner.

CHAPTER TWO

"Sorry, Hannah, I should have phoned beforehand but I was in the area and..." Claudia left the sentence unfinished as she watched Hannah unlocking the door and turning off the alarm as they went into the hall.

Hannah looked tired, Claudia thought, and after everything she'd been through it was little wonder. At least the security on her home appeared robust with the new, reinforced door and locks, plus a top of the range alarm system.

"Are you here about the body in the Pond? Sergeant Benton said it was a suicide." They had left Elizabeth dozing in her buggy in the hall as Hannah made coffee in the kitchen.

"Would seem so. Stones in her pockets, poor kid."

Hannah looked horrified. "A child?"

"No, a teenager, I think." Claudia seemed distracted for a moment then continued, "Anyway, as I said I was in the area so called in to tell you, before you saw anything on the news, that two more Somali girls have been found. A woman took them in to her local police station. We're not sure yet what the woman's connection to them is, if any. It seems they hadn't been harmed or abused but they're having a full medical check in hospital."

"And then?"

"Foster care, I suppose, until the authorities work out what to do with them."

"Be nice to think they could return to their families."

Claudia studied the other woman's face. "You don't sound very pleased."

Hannah handed her a mug of coffee and they sat at the kitchen table. The DI waited for her to say something. The silence was not a comfortable one. Hannah's investigation into her friend's death had uncovered an evil syndicate trafficking Somali girls into Europe and the US. Some high-profile people had been involved and had to resign from their various positions. But she feared that some of those who were masterminding the racket had not been caught or brought to justice.

"Believe me, I am pleased, Claudia. It's just that every time this comes up I think about how Liz died. This was why she died. And it hurts."

Claudia nodded. "I can imagine. But without your investigative work and perseverance, maybe none of the girls would have escaped. Think about that."

Hannah sipped her coffee. "I know. And I have so much to be grateful for as well." She looked away for a moment. "By the way did you ever find out what happened to Sherlock, that guy who took a bullet for me?"

Hannah's tone belied the terror she'd felt, standing on the steps of St John's church in Waterloo, suddenly confronted by the blinding flash of a camera and then the jostling around her. Voices shouting – commanding. The memory of the man who had moved in front of her so quickly and stood resolutely still although he had been hit by the bullet meant for her...

"Sorry, no." Claudia had flushed slightly. Hannah assumed she was lying but was in no mood to pursue it.

"It was strange seeing your sergeant, Mike Benton, in Peckham Park."

Claudia didn't comment.

"He looked different. Smartened himself up. Looks healthier too. Mind you his antipathy towards me hasn't changed."

Claudia laughed. "Two out of three isn't bad." It didn't escape Hannah's notice that she had offered no explanation.

They finished their coffee just as Elizabeth called out.

"I won't keep you. Why don't we catch up over a drink soon? I could come here if it makes it easier with babysitting?"

Hannah smiled. "That would be nice." Her lack of a social life meant that even a visit from Claudia was a welcome distraction.

They stood awkwardly, facing each other in the narrow hallway. Claudia touched Hannah's arm. "Take care, won't you?"

"Of course." Hannah closed the door behind her and let out a deep breath.

Now what was that all about, Hannah wondered as she sat down and had lunch with Elizabeth. Why should Claudia make a special visit to tell her about the Somali girls? Was she checking up on her? Had someone asked the DI to look in on her?

A half-eaten cherry tomato landing on her plate, followed closely by a shriek of laughter, ended all speculation. Elizabeth in her own inimitable way was right – she should focus on the here and now and count her blessings. Her daughter had also been a target. A fact that she would never forget.

CHAPTER THREE

Hannah finished keying in her copy and sat back from the computer, stretching her arms above her head. She smiled. This was definitely a feel-good story. A real TOT. Triumph over tragedy. Although in this case the tragedy had been averted. She'd been to interview a woman whose son was born prematurely weighing less than two pounds. Amazing. Seeing the little boy, Alistair, now at school and looking like any other energetic and adventurous five-year-old, was heart-warming.

Maybe *The News* editor, Georgina Henderson, was going soft, giving her this story. Or perhaps she was trying to edge her back to work gently. Her new contract meant she was tied to the newspaper, but it didn't specify how many articles she had to write, which seemed a trifle odd. However Rory assured her that it was in the newspaper's interest to keep her away from other news outlets. And them away from her. Hannah was happy with the arrangement. She didn't want to become the story. Her monthly fee had been increased so her finances were secure – for the time being.

Bizarrely, for the miracle baby feature, she had been paired up with Mike Laurel, the photographer she'd worked with on the first prostitute story at King's Cross. He'd just nodded at her when he arrived and, much to her astonishment, he was brilliant with the little boy. The photos were going to be stunning. The mother had blond hair cut in the style of *Friends* star Jenifer Aniston and was naturally good looking. Even so it was obvious she'd taken a lot of trouble over what she was wearing and her make-up was immaculate.

"I'll pop a set of prints in the post for you," Mike had said to her. That's nice, Hannah had thought; and then remembered how he'd probably sold on photos of Princess and given her an extra tenner for her trouble. Always an eye to the main chance.

"Can I give you a lift anywhere?" he'd asked as they left together.

Hannah hesitated. She preferred her own company but it was a long walk to the tube station in this north London suburb, and the quicker she got home the sooner she'd see Elizabeth.

"Thanks. I'd appreciate a lift to the station."

"I can do better than that," he said as he unlocked the car. "My next job's in Sydenham so I can drop you home en route."

Inwardly she groaned but forced a smile on to her face.

"Perfect, thank you."

As it turned out, Mike wasn't up for conversation either. As soon as they set off he turned on the radio. LBC. Not her favourite station but it did keep listeners up to date with any traffic problems.

They were crossing Blackfriars Bridge, when Mike said, "You've had a rum deal lately. How're you bearing up?"

"Okay – one day at a time." She forced herself to relax into the seat. The breathing exercises the doctor had given her helped too.

"Don't let yourself get bullied by that lot at *The News*. They may seem as though they're looking after you, but it's their own interests they're protecting."

"You seem to know a lot about it. What makes you the expert?" She knew how ungracious she sounded but she'd had enough of people giving her their opinion.

"Seen it all before." The smile he directed at her seemed more like a leer.

Good for you, Hannah thought but managed a tight smile. She wondered what, exactly, he'd seen before. Hardly likely to be that many journalists who'd escaped abduction, had a bomb planted in their house, and when that failed were shot at by a US hitman. But she said nothing.

They had reached the Elephant and Castle and miraculously the roads were clear. Not too much longer trapped in his car.

"I wouldn't trust that police officer you're friendly with either."

"Oh? Which one?" Hannah feigned indifference.

Mike crashed the gears as he changed down when the traffic lights moved to amber.

"I thought you were seeing that Tom Jordan guy?"

DI Tom Jordan – the man who had twice turned up to save her and Elizabeth's lives. Tom, the man who'd made her feel…

"I'd have a job, he's working in New York." Hannah smiled to cover the fact that she'd cheerfully like to wipe that supercilious smirk from Mike's face.

The lights changed. "Fancy a drink some time, then?"

By now they were at Camberwell Green. Hannah remained silent.

"Thought not. My loss."

The silence continued until they reached Lordship Lane.

"Could you drop me off here? I need to get a few things from the supermarket."

He slowed to a stop but had to double-park so Hannah could make a quick exit.

"Thanks for the lift, Mike."

"Pleasure. Let me know if you change your mind about that drink." He gave her a salute and was off.

Hannah crossed the road and went into the supermarket. Just in case he was watching her in the rear-view mirror.

Mike had made her feel unclean. She didn't like him and couldn't help feeling he was giving her some sort of warning. And it had only just occurred to her that he knew where she lived, or at least the area; and she certainly hadn't told him. Still that would have been easy to discover. She didn't find that thought reassuring.

Hannah reread what she had written and made a few changes, corrected a couple of typos. She decided to have a break before sending the story in. Plenty of time. Janet was playing with Elizabeth in the garden. She watched them from the window and smiled. More sand was being thrown around the lawn than was being used to build castles.

She made some coffee in her study rather than risk disturbing them from the kitchen. While Elizabeth didn't know she was in the house she was happy being with Janet, but she was getting to the demanding stage – when she saw her mother she wanted to stay with her.

Hannah checked her watch. Two o'clock. So nine in the morning in New York. Perhaps Tom had sent an email. She clicked on the dial-up for the Internet and waited for her emails to come through. Only one from Rory asking when her premature baby article would be ready.

Nothing from Tom. What was he working on that was so important to keep him in the US? A niggling thought crossed her mind that he was prolonging his stay. Maybe they didn't have a future and he was putting off telling her?

As she watched her own daughter playing in the garden, she thought about the teenager who had drowned in Peckham Pond. Her family must be devastated. There had been nothing on the news and Rory said he'd heard nothing when she asked him. Suicides obviously weren't high on the news agenda. Unless it was a celebrity or a public figure.

Her thoughts turned to the envelope which was burning a hole in her bag. Inside was a visiting order. To visit Paul Montague. The father of her child who had been involved in a plot against them. To his credit he had saved Elizabeth and Janet at the eleventh hour. But could she breathe the same air as a man who had involved himself with such a murderous syndicate?

In the years they had been together, she knew he'd sailed close to the wind on some of the deals he made. Although she was never quite sure what it was he actually did. Buying and selling he'd always said. How could she have been so wrong about someone? Had love blinded her? Now she wasn't even sure she had ever loved him. They'd had a fairly relaxed relationship. Liked doing similar things. Holidays were fun. However she realised there was something always missing. And when she became pregnant it became apparent. No real commitment.

Hannah finished her coffee. One last read through and she'd email her article to Rory then spend some quality time with Elizabeth. She wasn't going to waste her time worrying about Paul.

CHAPTER FOUR

"That sounded like a heartfelt sigh." Hannah had walked into the sitting room from the garden through the open French windows.

Linda was marking piles of books at the dining table. She looked up and smiled but her expression was tired and troubled.

"I was just thinking about how some girls don't stand a chance even in this day and age. It makes me want to weep…"

Hannah handed her a glass of wine and sat opposite her. "Looks like I arrived at an opportune time." She raised her glass. "What's the problem?"

Linda was quiet for a moment. "You know our daughters will still have to fight to be treated as equals in society but they won't have one arm tied behind their backs." She took a sip of wine. "I have a girl in my class who's really bright. She could do well in her GCSEs and go on to take A levels, maybe go to university. But she won't. She'll be lucky to scrape a D on her current performance."

Hannah studied her friend. It was unlike her to be so negative. She was a dedicated and inspired teacher, or so she always seemed.

"So what's holding her back?"

Linda closed an exercise book and scraped back her chair. The sound of the children playing in the garden with David filtered through. Such a beautiful and unexpectedly warm spring afternoon after a period of heavy showers.

"Her family. They come from India and have a huge network of relatives living here. If one of her younger cousins is ill, that auntie will phone and demand she looks after the child while she goes to work. Believe me it happens with monotonous regularity. This girl misses so many lessons. And when she is in school, she often struggles because she needs to catch up and she's tired. She has to help with all the cooking and cleaning at home. It's so unfair. Her brother is in the year above and he's a real high-flyer. Her two younger sisters are doing better."

"So can't the school do anything? Follow up on her absences and so on?"

"Believe me we've tried. Nothing works. She'll end up leaving school with virtually no qualifications and will be married off whether she likes it or not."

"What a depressing scenario." Hannah sipped her drink and stared out into the garden, lost in her own thoughts.

"You ought to write about it."

"What?" Hannah turned to focus on her friend. "Sorry I was miles away."

"The other side of the Atlantic?"

Hannah sighed. "Am I that transparent?"

"Yes." Linda paused and wondered if she should say anything more, but they had been friends for years. Sometimes the truth could be unpalatable. "One thing I've always admired about you is your resilience and how you focus on what's important. You cope with motherhood on your own brilliantly and in spite of everything that's happened recently you've bounced back."

"But – I know there's a but coming." Hannah could feel a flush creeping up her neck. It wasn't that she couldn't take criticism, it was the knowledge that Linda was justified in taking her to task.

"Well, yes. You seem to lack a sense of proportion regarding Tom. I know what you've been through has brought you together, but you haven't spent a lot of time in each other's company. You don't really know much about him." She smiled hoping to soften her comments. "You've always been so fiercely independent that it's weird seeing you distracted by..." Linda let the thought hover between them.

"I know what you're saying," Hannah said at last. "It's just he seemed to offer an alternative to..." She didn't want to say "being on my own" which sounded feeble.

"And he may well still do so." Linda placed her hand on her friend's arm. "but you can't put your life on hold. Waiting for something which might not happen."

Hannah stared into her wine glass. Tom and she hadn't really had the chance to discover if they really did have something going for them. She took a large gulp of her drink and remembered her mother's words: "No one will want to take on another man's child". That simply wasn't true. Lots of men became stepfathers. Then she remembered Caroline and what her stepfather had done to her. But her mother's situation was so different to her own.

"Which is why," Linda continued having warmed to her subject, "you should concentrate on something else. Like the plight of these young girls."

Hannah looked at her blankly.

"Hello. Earth to Hannah – the journalist who wrote that brilliant piece on FGM?"

Hannah flushed. Being reminded of that article made her think of Mia, James's cousin who had shared her own heart-rending and traumatic experiences. And had given her valuable information. She hadn't seen James recently and that hurt her more than she'd like to admit.

"But I don't know anything about these communities."

"'These communities'? Oh come on, Hannah. You're a journalist. What did you know about prostitutes? Or the homeless? Girl trafficking? Investigate. Do some digging."

Hannah knew Linda was right and with her new brief at *The News* – as a contributing editor – she had more say about what she wrote. And she was being encouraged to take on challenging subjects. *The News*, it seemed, liked her style and the other journalists seemed to accept her new role – however grudgingly – now that Judy Barton wasn't there to egg them on.

Judy had been transferred to work on the Scottish edition. Although she'd been the butt of the staff journalist's spitefulness, Hannah couldn't help feeling a bit sorry for her. She'd been one of Paul's victims as well and when push came to shove she'd alerted Georgina, the editor, about what was happening.

Hannah still felt nauseous when she remembered the

moment when she thought Elizabeth and Janet had been killed in an explosion...

"I suppose I could ask around. One of my neighbours is Indian. Well she's British, lived here all her life. Still it would be a starting point..."

"It would. Now, how about a top-up?"

Hannah passed her glass. As Linda poured more wine she asked, "Have you seen much of Joe since his elevation?"

Hannah laughed. Joe Rawlington's plan to stand for the local council had been turned on its head when a by-election was triggered by the sudden resignation of the sitting Tory MP soon after Hannah's exposé on the trafficking of young girls from Somalia into Europe. The reason Liz had been murdered. And Father Patrick. And Sam Lockwood. The trail of deaths that was supposed to have included her own. Hannah's laughter quickly faded at the memories.

Joe had been persuaded, somewhat reluctantly it had to be said, to contest the seat. And he had decided to come out about his sexuality. No skeletons in his cupboard. Much to his amazement, he won by a landslide. Tory policies were not popular and John Smith looked set to take over the keys to Number 10 at the next election. A new era was emerging and Joe fit the bill perfectly in spite of his reservations.

"No, but I'm going to meet him at the House next week. See how he is faring in his new surroundings." Hannah smiled at the thought. She was so pleased for him – and his new partner whom she still hadn't met.

"How about seeing me in mine?"

Hannah looked perplexed. Linda was so much part of her home and family she couldn't really imagine her anywhere else. Fortunately she realised how patronising that thought was and didn't give voice to it.

"You mean at school?"

"Yes. Why don't you come and give a talk about working as a journalist? I'm sure the pupils would be interested. I would."

Hannah hesitated only a moment. "Sounds like a plan – I'll be able to see what you're really like in front of a classroom full of kids instead of brandishing a red pen from behind a tower of exercise books."

Linda smiled. "I'll check out some dates and get back to you." She raised her glass. "My mission is accomplished."

CHAPTER FIVE

One of the men shoved her and her open-toed sandal caught on the uneven ground. She struggled to stay upright but had stopped fighting now. She had no energy left to resist. All she could do was pray – pray that it would be over quickly. Her body throbbed with pain in places she didn't know could feel such agony. Each breath brought a new spasm. Her shirt was torn and her trousers had been ripped apart. Her hair had been shorn. She had no will to live now. She was dead inside. Whatever else they did to her could not be worse than what she had already suffered.

She felt the prod of the ceremonial sword that they had used to chop off her hair. The tunnel must come to an end soon. She tried to remember where did it lead? Towards the pond in Sydenham woods?

What had she done that was so offensive that she should be abused in this way? She thought of her mother. Such a gentle kind woman. Beautiful. Her father, tall and proud. Handsome. Everyone said that.

Why hadn't they protected her? Where were they?

She fell. A sandaled foot kicked her in the groin. "Get up," the perpetrator hissed.

Rolling on to her hands and knees, she managed to stand and stagger forward. Her heart was drumming in her ears. Her nose was bleeding and she wiped a hand across her face, wincing as it touched one of the bruises on her cheek. She couldn't go on much further. What more could they do to her? She sank to her knees then toppled forward descending into oblivion.

The evening loomed before her. Elizabeth had gone off to sleep almost immediately and Hannah was left with that familiar half-empty feeling. Restless. A nameless energy within her that couldn't find an outlet. She gathered up the books she'd been reading with an exhausted toddler and put them on their shelf before picking up a novel she'd started the evening before. Somehow it held no allure for her now. Maybe a video? *The Remains of the Day*? Maybe not.

And there was nothing she fancied watching on television either. What was Tom doing now? She wished he wasn't so far away. Still no point in dwelling on his absence and making herself feel more miserable. That way madness lies.

How she envied Linda and David. Their lives seemed to dovetail into perfection, or as near to it as humanly possible; from her perspective anyway. It irked her that she made comparisons like this. She had never seen herself as part of a conventional married couple. When she'd discovered she was pregnant and Paul wanted her to have a termination she had chosen to be a single parent – it hadn't been forced upon her. And judging by what Paul had subsequently been up to she'd had a lucky escape. Briefly she wondered how he was coping. He was currently on remand in Brixton prison. His visiting orders were a thorn in her side. Why would he think she would even consider visiting him?

Her thoughts turned to Linda's suggestion that she

should give a talk to her pupils. That appealed to her but at the same time she found the idea terrifying. What if she couldn't hold their attention? Would her voice be loud enough?

The thought of a lecture hall full of teenagers sent her into a blind panic. Then she giggled to herself. After everything she'd faced, she shouldn't be intimidated by some stroppy pupils. She couldn't let the shadows blight her life. Linda was right.

The telephone rang. Hannah was tempted to let it go through to the answerphone but it might just be Tom. Not many friends rang her at this time on a Sunday evening. Not many friends full stop, she thought bitterly. She picked up the handset and a well-modulated voice with a hint of an accent Hannah couldn't identify asked to speak to her.

"Speaking."

"Good. My name is Sunita Kumar and I would very much like to meet with you." The name meant nothing to Hannah but the tone of voice made it sound like a royal summons.

"In what connection, Ms Kumar?"

"My niece who was found drowned in Peckham Rye Park. Would two-thirty tomorrow afternoon be convenient?"

"Ye-es." Hannah was intrigued.

Sunita Kumar gave her an address in Herne Hill and abruptly hung up.

Hannah was bemused by the woman's attitude. Still there could be a newsworthy story about the suicide. The journalist in her hoped there was, though the part of her that was a mother was appalled that she should have entertained such a thought.

Hannah searched through her videos again. Nothing interested her. She phoned James and got his paging service. No point in leaving a message. She needed to get a grip on her life – it couldn't just be motherhood and work. She wanted something more for herself. But what? Tom?

She went upstairs to her office and dialled up the internet connection. No emails. But that didn't stop her sending one.

CHAPTER SIX

"I assure you, Ms Weybridge, my niece did not commit suicide. Amalia had absolutely no reason, no reason at all, to take her own life."

The suppressed rage emanating from the other woman brought to mind Lady Rayman when Liz had been murdered. Sunita Kumar was not at all how she'd imagined the aunt of the teenager found drowned in Peckham Pond. She was in her late thirties or early forties and her dark hair, with a startling streak of grey at the front, was styled into a short bob. Her top and trousers looked bespoke, a silk scarf with an intricate pattern was draped about her neck and shoulders and various gold bangles adorned her wrists; but she wore no rings. She was elegance personified. Her grief, however, was like a chiffon cloud blurring her evanescence.

Hannah shifted awkwardly in the armchair. They were in one of the reception rooms of the house Sunita Kumar shared with her brother and sister-in-law in Herne Hill. The room, like the aunt, was elegant and beautifully proportioned. It was, she had been told, her sitting room. Its twin on the other side of the large, square entrance hall was her brother's. The décor was fashionably muted. The room was warm, almost too warm, with a faint smell of something spicy.

"I appreciate how hard this must be for you, Ms –"

"Do you? Do you indeed?" Her eyes blazed in fury. "Let me tell you, Amalia had a brilliant future ahead of her. A brilliant future. She had been accepted to study medicine at Oxford. Why would she kill herself? And in such a way? I just cannot believe it." She studied Hannah's face. "And I know what you are thinking."

Hannah's confusion must have been apparent.

"That suicide by drowning is common in India. That..."

"Is it? I had no idea."

Sunita Kumar stood up and walked towards the window. Hannah's hope that she might open it was not fulfilled. The aunt returned to her seat and stared at Hannah.

"I am so sorry but it does seem that your niece intended to take her own life. She had weighted her clothes with stones –" Ms Kumar dismissed this with a wave of her hand. "However –"

"However?" Ms Kumar's face brightened at this glint of hope. The crack in the wall of bleakness.

"However, I can, if you would like me to, make some enquiries. But I can't promise you that the answers will be any different."

"You come highly recommended, Ms Weybridge."

Did she indeed? Hannah assumed Claudia had landed her with this to get the distraught woman off her own back.

"And when I spoke with Lady Rayman she..."

"I'm sorry, am I missing something here?"

"I've no idea what you may or may not be missing."

"You mentioned Lady Rayman."

"Yes. I am a trustee of the charity Lady Rayman set up in honour of her daughter. She suggested I contact you."

Hannah sent out a silent sorry to Claudia.

"I see." Hannah let the silence stretch between them.

"Amalia's parents – my brother and his wife – were too distraught to contact you but they have given me their permission to offer you whatever it costs." She reached across and clasped Hannah's hand. "We really do need your help, Ms Weybridge."

Hannah understood her sorrow and grief and wondered if her regret would be worse if she didn't help this woman? "In that case let's start by you calling me Hannah."

"And please call me Sunita." The other woman's relief was palpable.

"If you would like me to look into this, as a journalist, I cannot accept any payment from you. And you have to be prepared for the fact that any investigation may uncover things you'd rather not know and would prefer not to see printed in a newspaper."

"I would rather know everything, however unpalatable, than to know nothing. To have this uncertainty. This…" She gave up trying to describe her feelings.

"Do you have anything for me to go on?"

Sunita went over to a chest of drawers and came back with an embroidered tote bag. "I have Amalia's diary, her school reports. We've made a list of her close friends at school."

Hannah glanced at the sheet of paper Sunita handed her, which was headed by the name of a local independent girls' school known for the academic achievements of its students.

"We shall also write to the Head Teacher, giving her our permission to reveal anything that may be relevant."

"Thank you, Sunita. I'll make an appointment with the Head and take it from there. But you know it really does look like Amalia…"

"I know, we know, what it looks like. But appearances can be deceptive, as you yourself have reason to believe."

Hannah wasn't quite sure what Sunita meant by that. The aunt handed her a copy of the post mortem report. Privately she didn't think she'd be able to add anything to what the investigation and post mortem had so far revealed: *Amalia Kumar had filled her pockets and clothes with stones and had willingly walked into the lake in Peckham Park with the deliberate intention of drowning herself.*

"Who identified Amalia's body?"

Sunita studied her hands. Hannah noticed her fingernails were cut short and looked recently manicured. Sunita, just like Celia Rayman, did not let standards slip, no matter how distressed she was. "I did. My brother and sister-in-law… I was anxious to spare them further grief." She inhaled deeply. "I was very close to my niece, but obviously not more so than her parents," she added hurriedly. "I just can't accept or understand why she wouldn't have spoken to me about anything, anything at all, that was worrying her."

Both women were silent.

"Are there any siblings?" Hannah asked.

"No." Sunita wrung her hands. "Sadly not."

As an only child herself, Hannah wondered if it was worse for parents when you lost that child. Liz too had been an only. Her own child would probably remain so… She cut short her thoughts.

"Did you see the police photographs taken at the scene?"

The aunt nodded. "Not something I would wish on my worst enemy."

"I don't wish to be insensitive, Sunita, but was there anything at all, apart from the obvious, that seemed strange to you."

Sunita had produced a lace handkerchief and was dabbing her eyes. "No. Nothing." The woman gazed into the distance. Then Hannah realised she was staring at a framed photograph of a young woman who, she assumed, was Amalia.

"She wasn't wearing her ring." The words came out like an exhalation of breath.

"I'm sorry?"

"She wasn't wearing the ring I had made especially for her on her sixteenth birthday. She never took it off."

"Maybe she did this time because of..."

"No. It certainly wasn't in her room. I was there when the police went through everything."

Hannah remained silent.

"I think they were looking for a suicide note. But of course there wasn't one."

"I could contact the police, on your behalf, just in case they have it among her possessions?"

"But I saw photographs of her hands. She definitely wasn't wearing her ring."

"Perhaps it came off in the water."

Sunita was shaking her head even before Hannah had finished her question.

"Do you have a good photograph of the ring I could

have? And one of Amalia?"

"There is a photograph in the bag." She stood up and walked over to an ornate writing table and came back with an envelope which she handed to Hannah. Inside were two photographs of the ring, one showing the simple inscription: *Amalia with all my love Sunita.* Another sheet of paper bore the name and address of the jeweller.

"Thank you." Hannah paused. She remembered Tom's advice when she'd told him she was investigating Liz's death for Lady Rayman. "One thing you could do, Sunita, is to arrange for a second post mortem. Sometimes things are overlooked, but –"

The aunt snatched at the suggestion. "I'll get on to that straight away. Thank you."

Hannah stood up and held out her hand. "My sincere condolences, Sunita. I'll get back to you as soon as possible."

Back at home in her study, Hannah mulled over the facts that she had been given. Amalia Kumar had been reported missing when she'd failed to return home after a late piano lesson at school. Her distraught parents had been told to wait. She was seventeen, may have gone off with a friend ... Her body had been found in Peckham Pond the next morning. The day Hannah had been walking through the park and ran into DS Mike Benton. She had apparently been in the water for some hours.

Why had she gone to Peckham Park? Why not Dulwich Park? There was a lake there as well. It was nearer her school and it would have been easy to find a place to hide until the gates were locked.

According to the post mortem, she had not been assaulted in any way and was still a virgin. Small comfort for her family, thought Hannah. To all intents and purposes, it looked as though she had indeed weighted her body with stones and deliberately drowned herself.

Hannah shuddered. How long did it take to die? Wouldn't the body's innate will to survive overcome suicidal thoughts? It seemed a terrible way to end one's life. But then the thought of ending one's own life was totally alien to her. No wonder Sunita Kumar refused to believe her niece had taken her own life in this way. But if she didn't kill herself, how did she die? And why?

CHAPTER SEVEN

"Hannah." Tom's voice was loud and clear after the initial pause of the transatlantic call. "How are you?"

"I'm fine. All things considered." A tightness in her throat made speaking difficult. His voice evoked a miasma of memories. Her body relived the comfort of his strong arms around her. Then she remembered his coolness when they had parted. He'd seemed indifferent to her then as he left to return to the States.

"Did Graham sort out the security for you?" Tom spoke as though they had seen each other yesterday.

"Yes, he's been such a help. I didn't know half of these things existed."

Tom chuckled then sounded serious. "I wish you didn't have to know they did."

"Well it's very reassuring to have them and it does mean I can stay here. If anyone's going to come after me..."

"They won't." Tom's voice was harsh.

"Well they would find me wherever I am, so I might as well be here."

Neither of them spoke of the reason for heightened security but it hung there between them as if suspended on a telephone wire, swaying gently. Hannah knew that MI5 had stepped in to round up the syndicate who were trafficking the Somali girls in the UK. She had been told to be vigilant – just in case... She assumed that meant just in case some of the ringleaders were still at large.

Just in case another hit-man from the US arrived and

found his target this time? Presumably the FBI was also making arrests. She sincerely hoped so.

"I'm hoping to be finishing up here soon." Tom's tone was hesitant. "When my secondment finishes I should be back in London. Not sure in what capacity yet."

Hannah was silent.

"Hannah I ... I would like us to be able to get to know each other properly. I'd like..."

"Yes I'd like that too." They both laughed. The tension between them eased fractionally.

"Do you think we can try to put all the past horrors behind us? Do normal things and not be trying to right the injustices of the world."

"Perhaps," said Hannah. "I do have my new contract at *The News*." He made a sound that Hannah couldn't or didn't want to interpret. "Lord Gyles has been so supportive and it does mean other news outlets can't get access to me. It's a protection of sorts."

Tom's silence was eloquent. She knew he had mixed feelings about her newspaper connections. But then she wasn't sure what she thought about what Tom was or wasn't involved in. He was always so evasive. Presumably he'd signed the Official Secrets Act. But that could be a cover for so many things.

"Actually," she said on a more conciliatory note, "I think the editor has gone soft on me. Sent me off to interview a mother whose son weighed only two pounds when he was born prematurely and is now a healthy five-year-old. Women's mag stuff."

"Sounds safe."

"Mmm – you've met the photographer; he was the

one I worked with on the King's Cross story."

Tom said nothing, perhaps remembering her interview with him and the murders of prostitutes that had first brought them together.

When he spoke Hannah thought she could hear a catch in his voice. "I don't ever want to see another gun pointed at you or Elizabeth."

Hannah breathed deeply, her memories too raw.

"We could have a holiday? Time to relax together?"

"Sounds perfect. I'll be due some leave. I'll let you know as soon as I can about my return date."

"Okay. Tom, it will be so good to see you."

"You too. Give a hug to Elizabeth for me."

"I will."

As if on cue, as she put the phone down, Janet returned with the toddler screeching, "Mama! Mama! Come see me."

And Hannah was back in her world.

CHAPTER EIGHT

Why would an A grade student with everything to look forward to take her own life? Hannah had been to the school and the Head, Dr Stella Landcroft, confirmed that she'd had no problems, or none the school had any knowledge of. Hannah wondered how aware the school staff was of their students' private problems and anxieties. Perhaps she was being unfair.

"Amalia was a popular girl, Ms Weybridge. She was intelligent, diligent in her studies, a team player. She also did some voluntary work at the local hospice."

"Sounds like the perfect student."

Dr Landcroft peered at her over her glasses. Her steely grey eyes reflected her severe expression. "Asian girls who attend this school usually come from families where the parents are professional people. So they support and nurture their daughters' aspirations. Our girls are encouraged and stretched but never beyond their capabilities. Amalia did not take her own life because of academic concerns, I assure you."

"No, I agree that seems unlikely." Hannah paused. "Do you think she could have been bullied?"

Dr Landcroft glared at her. "Certainly not, we have a robust anti-bullying policy at this school. Bullying in any shape or form is not and will never be tolerated."

Hannah wondered why the woman was so blatantly hostile. Protesting too much? "Amalia's aunt gave me a list of some of her friends. Would it be possible to speak with them? Chaperoned, of course," Hannah added seeing the frown on the Head Teacher's face.

"Ms Weybridge, I am aware of the investigative work you have done for *The News*." She pronounced the name of the newspaper as though someone has waved something unsavoury under her nose. "I admire how you've handled some of the more sensitive exposés." The compliment seemed to have been wrenched from her. "However, I can assure you there is nothing untoward going on in this establishment. Nothing that will interest your readers."

Hannah smiled and tried to look as placatory as she could. "I'm not here as a journalist, Dr Landcroft –" she metaphorically crossed her fingers – "but as an advocate for Amalia's family. They are convinced – contrary to all evidence, I grant you – that she didn't take her own life. I'm just exploring all avenues for them."

"Quite." She looked at her watch. "It's break in a few minutes. I've already asked the girls to meet you in the upper sixth common room. Mrs Conway, our head of year 13, will be there as an appropriate adult."

"Thank you very much for your time, Dr Landcroft."

Hannah stood up as the Head commanded "Enter," in response to a knock on her door. She smiled at the girl. "Thank you, Sophia. Please accompany Ms Weybridge to the common room."

The girl smiled at her. "If you'd like to follow me, Ms Weybridge?"

Hannah shook hands with the Head and followed the girl.

Looking at her notes later, Hannah couldn't see one

remotely possible reason why Amalia would commit suicide. As far as was possible to judge, she certainly wasn't being bullied. She was cherished at home by both parents and aunt. She hadn't left a note or any clue as to what had driven her to such an extreme act.

Her friends were deeply shocked and subdued. Hannah thought she saw a hint of fear in the two Asian students' eyes. But that might just have been her imagination. Go back to facts, she told herself.

So:

Amalia Kumar DOB: 12 June, 1976

School: excellent and gifted student

Parents: supportive (I assume) given aunt's stance

Aunt: cannot come to terms with a suicide?

Manner of death – why would she have chosen drowning?

As she had been about to leave the sixth form common room, a girl came up to her. She spoke quietly, rapidly as though trying to get her words out before courage deserted her.

"I saw Amalia having an argument with a man outside school one afternoon."

"What sort of man?" Hannah was intrigued. "Young? Old? Could he have been a boyfriend?"

"I don't think so. He looked … well he looked threatening. And at one point he grabbed Amalia's hand, but she pulled away from him and came back into school."

"Sensible girl. Go on." Hannah was making notes as the girl spoke.

"I asked her what that was all about and she said," the girl paused. "She said 'Just some creep who should know better.' That's all. Then a group of us left the building together and she got on the no.37 bus home."

"Thank you –?"

"Harriet."

"Thank you Harriet. When was this?"

Harriet's eyes welled up with tears. "The day before she died. I'm sorry. Maybe if I'd said something..." The girl blinked rapidly and tore at the screwed-up tissue in her hand.

Hannah touched her shoulder. "Please don't torture yourself. That encounter could have been nothing to do with Amalia's death. Here's my card in case you remember anything else. You've been really helpful."

The girl pushed back her strawberry blond curls from her face and sniffed loudly. "Sorry."

"Is there someone here you feel you can talk to?"

"Not really. I tried to tell our form tutor about that man, but she said I'd exaggerated it."

"Did she?" Hannah was struggling not to say what she really thought. "Well I don't think you were exaggerating. Ring me if you or any of the other girls think of anything unusual about Amalia before she died."

The girl nodded. "Shall I walk you back to reception?"

"Thank you." Hannah smiled and followed Harriet out of the room, aware that the sixth form tutor's eyes had never left them and she did not look pleased. Now why was that?

CHAPTER NINE

The pathologist who undertook the second post mortem was the same one Lady Rayman had used. Hannah assumed the two women had conferred. Dr Matthew Carter phoned Hannah first as Sunita Kumar had instructed him to do. With little preamble he launched into his findings.

"Obviously the death was caused by drowning and it looks like suicide from the description of how she'd weighted her clothes and body."

There was a pause. "However I did find a tiny thread in her mouth. And a slight sticky residue on her upper lip. This may lead to nothing but if there was concern that she had been coerced into taking her own life, I would suggest that these two findings could be due to a gag being placed in her mouth and then held in place with duct tape which was removed prior to her drowning."

Hannah was silent absorbing these facts. She felt sick.

"Ms Weybridge?"

"Yes, I'm sorry I was thinking about what you just said."

"There's more." Hannah could hear the rustle of paper. "I also found the slightest of abrasions on her left wrist. This may have been caused by having her wrists tied with something soft but strong. Like silk."

"So she could have been taken to the lake by force and then..."

"Pure conjecture, but someone or some persons could have induced her to drown herself."

"Which would be murder."

"Exactly." Dr Carter coughed. "Ms Kumar asked me to contact you with my findings in the first instance. Shall I fax or email them to you and leave you to deal with the results?" He sounded relieved that he didn't have to speak to the grief-stricken aunt.

"Yes. Thank you. Email – you have my address."

"I do. Well good luck with your investigations." He hung up leaving Hannah feeling stunned and confused. She'd have to think carefully about what she'd say to Sunita Kumar. But she also needed to inform the police.

DI Claudia Turner answered her mobile on the third ring. "Turner."

"Hi Claudia, have you got a moment? I need a favour."

"Go on."

"I need to know what has happened about Amalia Kumar who was found drowned in Peckham Park?"

"The suicide? I assume the file has been sent to the coroner. Why?"

"I have some new evidence from a second post-mortem which suggests it may not have been suicide."

Hannah thought she heard a mumbled, "You would, wouldn't you". There was a sigh. "Okay why don't you forward me the report and we'll take it from there."

"Thanks. And one other thing."

"Go on."

"Did you find a rather distinctive ring? Amalia wasn't wearing it in the photos, but her aunt is convinced she would have been."

"Well I'll check that out. I'm assuming you have a

photo of it for me?"

"Yes – I thought it might be worth checking out the Peckham pawn shops."

"Grandmothers and eggs, Hannah. Grandmothers and eggs." And with that she hung up.

Hannah clicked on the dial up Internet connection. It was always slower in the afternoon after the US had woken up. She always checked for emails from Tom but there was rarely anything.

The report had come in from the pathologist. She read it slowly, absorbing the implications and what it might mean for the family. Sunita had been vindicated in her suspicions. But what good would that do her? It wouldn't bring her niece back. Then she chided herself. Of course it would be better not to think that someone close to you had deliberately ended her life and you had no idea why.

Hannah copied the report and pasted it into an email to Claudia, then checked for any work emails. There was one from Rory asking when she'd be in the office next as he had an idea to discuss with her. She replied saying she'd be in later that day. Then she called and arranged to meet Sunita.

The room was just as she remembered it except there seemed to be more photos of Amalia, most in silver frames on top of the mahogany chests of drawers and cupboards. Sunita had answered the door and led her into the room without a word.

"My brother and his wife are still too distraught to

see anyone," she replied to the question Hannah hadn't asked.

"And how are you bearing up, Sunita?"

"My anger keeps me going. Now what do you have for me?" She indicated a seat for Hannah who sank into the deep cushions and wished they could swallow her up rather than face this woman's anguish.

Hannah removed an envelope from her handbag. "I have the second post mortem report." Hannah was unsure whether she should say more or just hand over the report she'd printed out. In the end she let Sunita read it for herself without comment.

"I knew it. She didn't kill herself." She looked terrifying. Fury burned in her eyes. Then suddenly tears poured down her face unchecked. Hannah felt uncomfortable witnessing such raw, silent grief.

She pulled out a packet of tissues and handed them to Sunita without comment. The other woman blew her nose and wiped her hands across her face. "I do apologise for my lack of restraint, Hannah."

"Please don't. Sometimes it's good to let go for a moment."

"Yes, I suppose it is." She sniffed. "So where do we go from here?"

"Well, I've forwarded this report on to the police. To Detective Inspector Turner."

Sunita shook her head. "I don't know this Detective Inspector. We were informed of Amalia's death by a Sergeant Benton. He seemed competent but… what will the police do?"

Hannah was surprised at the bitterness of her tone.

"An Asian girl getting herself killed isn't top of their priorities, is it?"

Hannah's face must have betrayed her shock.

"They are racist, Hannah. We face prejudice all the time."

The 'but' she was about to pronounce stuck in Hannah's throat.

"They will not investigate in the same way as they would if it was a white British girl."

"Then we'll have to make sure they do, won't we?"

Sunita glared at her for a moment then her face relaxed. She actually managed a smile. "Celia told me how tenacious you are. I know you put yourself at risk to expose Liz's killers. But she was your close friend. That was your motivation. We are strangers to you."

Hannah said nothing for a moment. "The Somali girls who were trafficked were unknown to me. Yet I don't regret for one moment that I put myself on the line for them." She looked across at the large photo of Amalia now adorned with a garland of silk flowers. "I do however regret exposing my own daughter to extreme danger. I could never do that again."

"And nor should anyone ask that of you." Sunita clasped her hand and smiled. "Never again. But I should be eternally grateful if your investigations could prompt the police to find Amalia's killer."

CHAPTER TEN

The shrill sound of the whistle caused everyone to stop in their tracks. No one spoke. Above them crows circled. Bluebells nodded silently in the gentle spring breeze. Sunlight filtered through the ancient treetops of Dulwich Woods.

"Over here."

Three figures moved through the undergrowth to the officer at the left of the line. Shock bleached his face.

Looking down they saw what in all probability had been dislodged by a fox from its long term resting place. The visible part of the skull was dirty with a fragment of fabric still attached in some way.

The four officers stared at the ground and then each other. This was obviously not the missing girl they were searching for.

"Shit. Sorry Sarge." The constable who had spoken let out a low whistle. "Not exactly what we were expecting. God knows how long this one's been here."

As he spoke members from the scene of crime team, who had been on standby, were ready to mark out the area and take photographs. Within minutes a tent was erected over the site.

The shout went out for the officers to continue their painstaking task of exploring the area for any clue as to the whereabouts of the schoolgirl who had been reported missing twenty-seven hours previously.

Nadia Chopra, aged fifteen, had not turned up for school. But her attendance record was such that no one checked where she was. It was her mother's frantic 999 call that had sparked the search. The distraught mother could hardly speak English so DS Benton interviewed her with her twelve-year old son acting as an interpreter. It crossed the sergeant's mind that the boy wasn't translating exactly what his mother said. She looked perplexed at times, repeatedly interrupting, saying "No, no Pashi," but her son just said something in their language and Benton was none the wiser. He made a mental note to arrange for a professional interpreter to be present if they had to interview her again.

The search party had neared the pond that was covered with black gunge. Before anyone knew what was happening one of the police dogs had plunged in. His trainer called and whistled to no avail. The officers nearest the edge stood stock still in mute horror as the dog dived then slowly pushed what looked like a bag of sodden rags to the edge.

As the water and plants moved around the bundle, a hand became visible. Then the bundle flipped over. A face stared unseeingly up at the sky, the eyes already a delicacy for some creature below...

Nadia had been found.

DS Benton radioed into the station. "I'll need an interpreter," he said after explaining that they'd found, they assumed, the body of Nadia Chopra. "One who speaks Punjabi. And pronto. Yeah I'll wait."

Mike wandered over to where a group of officers had gathered. They looked as he felt. Shocked and sick. He thought back to the body of Amalia Kumar that they'd found in Peckham Park. In comparison she looked like the Lady of Shalott. Nadia had the appearance of having gone more rounds than you could count with Lennox Lewis. Added to which her hair had been shorn off ... no attempt had been made to make this look like a suicide. If, that is, there was any connection between the deaths of the two girls.

He thought back to the hysterical mother who had reported her daughter missing and the interview conducted in part via her twelve-year-old son. His gut reaction had been that something was not right in that household and he was going to make it his business to find out what it was.

His radio crackled. The interpreter would meet him outside Nadia's parents' house. When he saw the interpreter he was relieved it was Sonia Arora, someone he'd worked with before. The interview ahead was going to be difficult and Benton certainly didn't want the young brother in the room.

CHAPTER ELEVEN

Rory was at his desk going through some page proofs. He'd had to clear a space among the piles of press releases, newspapers and half-empty coffee cups. He smiled as Hannah approached him.

"What?" she asked.

"You've got that look about you."

"Which is?"

"Which is, 'I'm just about to ask some questions and it might just lead us to a major story'."

"Don't hold your breath then." She felt relaxed with Rory who had always supported her and gave her enough leeway to find herself in whatever she was researching. "But I do want to run something past you."

"Excuse me, Ms Contributing Editor, you don't have to do that." From someone else that comment may have sounded snide but Hannah knew Rory had been pleased at her new contract, and, she was sure, had had some influence in instigating it.

"Fancy lunch later?"

"Half an hour?" Hannah nodded and went back to her desk to make a cuttings request: anything on arranged marriages, disappearances of young Asian girls and unexplained or unusual suicides in the Asian community. Something about Amalia's death and Linda's absentee pupil niggled. Were they both part of a bigger picture?

They were early so managed to get a table in the corner of the Pen and Ink public house. Rory ordered a pint of best for himself, white wine for Hannah and some ham sandwiches. Their usual fare. While they were waiting for their order to arrive, Rory produced a photocopied cutting. It was dated two days previously from South Africa. Hannah's vision blurred as the name Gerry Lacon jumped out at her.

Rory put his hand over hers. "He's dead, Hannah. It's been reported as natural causes but reading between the lines it looks like he was got at. That was always on the cards given his track record over there." He smiled. "And it could be some people need to clear the decks before Mandela gets sworn in on Tuesday. Anyway, one less demon to haunt you."

Hannah took a gulp of the wine. Dead. Gerry Lacon, the man who had held a gun to her baby's head. The man who had ordered Caroline – and the others – killed. Poetic justice perhaps? For a moment she thought of Sarah, his wife. Had they divorced? She had no idea. No good dwelling on the past.

She realised that Rory was obviously waiting for her to say something. "Thanks. As you say one less demon..."

Their sandwiches arrived and between mouthfuls Rory filled her in about Judy Burton and her plea to George – no one called Georgina this to her face – to return to London. She obviously wasn't enjoying her exile in Scotland.

"Oh, I thought she would have found her Celtic roots by now." Hannah winked. "I thought she'd find Scotsmen in kilts irresistible."

Rory looked about to choke.

"At least I don't have to make that decision," Hannah said.

"And what decisions do you have to make, then?"

Hannah stared across the bar. For a moment she thought she saw Paul standing there, looking across at her. She blinked and he was gone. In his place was a man who vaguely resembled him.

"You look as though you've seen a ghost."

"Maybe I have." Hannah finished her wine.

"Another?" Rory asked and she nodded, glad for his departure for a few moments. Maybe it was the mention of Judy, which had conjured up Paul's image.

"So – decisions," he said returning with their drinks.

"A friend of mine who's a teacher told me about how some young Asian girls are being taken out of school to look after members of their families. Some, it seems, are being forced into arranged marriages at a very young age."

"Sounds right up your street. What's the problem?"

"Not sure I should involve myself and the newspaper."

"Why? These girls are British citizens. Don't they deserve your support?"

Hannah was surprised at Rory's reaction. "What do you know about this then?"

"More than you may think. A cousin of mine married into an Indian family. Don't get me wrong, her in-laws are great but neither she nor I would say the same about some of the extended family."

Hannah sipped her drink. "Well I've called the cuttings service, so I'll see what comes up there." Hannah circled her glass over a damp patch on the table. "There is something else."

"Knowing you, Hannah, there always is." He grinned at her.

"There was a drowning in my local park. A young Asian girl. The police wrote it off as suicide but the family was convinced otherwise. The aunt asked me to look into it and a second post mortem suggested that she may have been coerced into drowning herself."

"Sounds a bit far-fetched. Why did the aunt contact you?"

"She's a trustee of the charity Celia Rayman set up in Liz's memory. Apparently she recommended me."

Rory finished his beer. "Well she could have done worse. Why don't you write that story first? Seems we have a scoop – such as it is. It obviously hasn't been picked up anywhere."

"No, the local press only reported the suicide. Also, a valuable and distinctive ring has gone missing – I have good images of that and it may jolt someone's memory."

"Good." Rory finished his pint. "Any plans for the weekend?"

"Seeing friends and being an attentive mother. You?"

"Need you ask?" Hannah looked at him blankly. "West Ham are playing Southampton and I have tickets. But for now it's back to the coal face."

"Is this guy for real?" John, one of the younger news reporters was shaking his head.

Hannah looked up from the cuttings she was studying. "Who?"

"His name is Peter Marks. He is, apparently, a private

investigator, who would like to discuss some possible news story ideas."

"Oh yes." Rory had walked back into the office. "And what might they be?"

"He says he has intelligence on how security services in South Africa infiltrated a high security prison in order to perpetrate a revenge killing."

Rory looked across at Hannah whose face had drained of colour. "Well I don't suppose that was too difficult to effect given the resources of the NIS."

"This guy Peter Marks reckons he was part of the team."

"Does he now?" Rory was leafing through a battered leather Filofax he'd retrieved from his desk drawer. "Thought so. He's also a bit-part actor and singer... okay John, arrange a meeting with him and see what he's got to offer."

John looked bemused.

"We'll pay him for exclusive rights to his info and it'll go into the vault, but we won't tell him that, of course."

Hannah could feel her face redden. Her own story had been spiked. Caroline's story. And Gerry Lacon had been part of that. She had to shake herself to remember that they had not spiked her exposé about the trafficking of Somali girls. That one had been reported... Eventually. But at what cost?

CHAPTER TWELVE

"You've cut your hair!" He was outside her house, leaning against a car, smiling and relaxed. Looking for all the world as though they had seen each other the day before and had not spent the last weeks communicating via the odd email and transatlantic call.

Hannah's hand immediately touched her hair as though in confirmation. She opened her mouth but no words emerged as she was engulfed by his embrace.

Tom stood back and grinned. "Thought I'd surprise you."

"Well you've certainly done that." Hannah could hear the sharpness in her tone. What was wrong with her? How many times had she dreamed of him turning up just like this? Out of the blue? And now that he had, she felt put out and irritated. She stepped back and rummaged in her bag for the door keys.

"Perhaps Elizabeth will be more welcoming."

Hannah could feel him watching her as she unlocked the reinforced door and keyed in the code to turn off the alarm. He followed her into the hall. "Hannah, I'm sorry. I had to come to London for a briefing and managed to add on a couple of days' leave. I thought it would be a happy surprise – not an unwelcome one."

"You're not unwelcome, it's just... Oh I don't know. Coffee?"

They walked into the kitchen and Hannah filled the kettle. "Janet will be back with Elizabeth soon. They go to soft play on a Friday afternoon."

Tom smiled. Soft play. He longed for the ordinariness those words conjured up. "Do you have any plans for the weekend?"

"Why?" Hannah busied herself with the coffee pot and mugs.

"I was going to suggest a couple of nights away. By the sea. I thought... Hannah, what is it?"

Hannah walked over to the back door, unlocked it and walked outside. She inhaled deeply, the scents of her garden a heady mix of early roses and lavender. She could sense Tom hesitating, not knowing whether to follow her or not. He remained in the kitchen and, when the kettle boiled, she heard him making the coffee.

She was sitting at the white garden table and smiled as he approached with the coffee pot and mugs on a tray.

"Sorry, my emotions are all over the place at the moment. So much seems to be happening and then nothing changes. Did you hear about Gerry Lacon?"

It seemed an odd question. But Lacon linked them back to Caroline and their first meeting. There were misunderstandings between them then and they had survived those pretty well – in the end. "Yes I did." He poured the coffee and passed her a mug.

They drank in an uncomfortable silence.

"So what do you think?"

Hannah looked away. "About what? Gerry Lacon's death?"

"No! A weekend away? By the sea?"

Hannah thought about the weekend that had stretched before her. Time in the park with Elizabeth. Pottering about the house and garden together. Playing. And then the long evenings when her precious daughter was safely tucked up in bed and she was left at a loose end.

"It sounds lovely. I haven't got anything planned that can't be rescheduled." That made it sound like a business arrangement. What was she thinking of?

A commotion from within the house and an imperious call of "Mama?" broke into the tense atmosphere. Hannah went into the kitchen, had a hurried conversation with Janet and then reappeared with Elizabeth in her arms.

"Look who's come to see us." Elizabeth hid her face in her mother's neck. "It's Tom."

Slowly, the child's face emerged and she stared at the man in the garden. "Tom," she repeated and smiled at him but with no hint of recognition.

"Hello, Elizabeth." Tom had a special timbre in his voice when he spoke to the child and it seemed to click with some memory. Her face lit up; she kissed her mother, then wriggled free and toddled over to Tom.

"Hello Tom."

Tom said he had some calls to make so Hannah left him in the sitting room while she bathed Elizabeth and put her into her nightclothes for the journey. Janet had already packed the essentials for Elizabeth and it didn't take Hannah long to fill her own bag with what she regarded as 'holiday' clothes and her toiletries. Since the explosion that had been meant to kill her, Hannah always had a bag of essentials at the ready just in case they ever needed to make a hasty departure. It was one of her coping mechanisms. There were others less obvious but just as reassuring. Like having cash and an extra credit card locked in her desk at *The News*. She also had a bag of essentials and another card stored with Linda and David.

Janet had left with a cheery wave and a bag of items from the fridge that Hannah asked her to use up as they'd be away.

Finally they were in the car Tom had hired and were off. Elizabeth, strapped into her car seat in the back, soon nodded off to the music Tom had switched on.

"I've booked us into the Queen's in Brighton. It's near the front and is fairly anonymous. Is that ok?"

"Mmm, not sure it will be up to our last hotel experience."

Tom looked nonplussed.

"My weak attempt at a joke, I'm afraid. Lord Gyles paid for us to stay at the Dorchester when…" her voice broke, "when…"

Tom reached for her hand. Hannah absorbed its warmth knowing there was nothing he could say without sounding trite and appreciating his sympathetic silence. He moved his hand to change gear. Soon they were out of the south London suburbs.

Miraculously for a Friday evening, the A3 had been relatively fast flowing but he'd spotted what seemed like an accident up ahead and took the slip road off to bypass it. As he did do he glanced in the mirror and saw that the car he thought had been tailing them had followed. He wondered which of them – Hannah or himself – was under surveillance. Maybe both. As soon as he saw a pub, he pulled over into the car park.

Hannah looked at him, then at the child sleeping in the back.

"No problem, just need to check something in the boot. Thought I heard a rattle."

Tom released the boot lock then got out of the car. The vehicle that he suspected was following them was forced to carry on or risk being exposed. But Tom now had the registration number. He made a quick call on his mobile out of Hannah's earshot and then returned to the car.

CHAPTER THIRTEEN

DS Benton knocked on DI Turner's office door and entered. The room was bare of anything personal save a suit in a plastic shroud hanging on the back of the door. No photos on the desk. No citations on the walls. She was, or liked to give the appearance of being, a closed book. However Benton had reason to grateful for her pastoral care. Their relationship had improved over the last few months. He'd got his act together and appreciated the faith she now had placed in him.

Claudia smiled as he entered. "How'd it go?"

"Grim." He sat down in the chair opposite her.

She opened her desk drawer and produced a bottle of scotch and two glasses. She poured and passed one to Benton.

He gulped a mouthful. "The mother was totally hysterical and the father appeared torn apart by the news. Everyone in the family has a cast iron alibi. But…"

"But? Come on Mike, what's your gut instinct?"

"That something isn't right. It feels as though they're concealing something. The interpreter thought the same. It's not what they said or didn't say but rather the way they appeared utterly defeated. As though they had known their daughter's murder was going to happen."

Claudia sipped her drink. "Go on."

"When I took the father to identify the body, he completely broke down. Went to pieces. The interpreter didn't come with us as Mr Chopra's English is very good. He said something, I couldn't understand. When I asked him he just shook his head and repeated it." Benton loosened his tie.

"Well let's run some background checks. See if any of their neighbours know anything of interest. Let's hope they're the nosey kind." Claudia looked down at the photos spread out on her desk. "Completely different MO to Amalia Kumar's murder."

"If it was."

"Oh, I think it was and Hannah Weybridge has made sure we'd look at the case again… She'll have an article in *The News* soon. Maybe that will dredge up something."

Even Benton looked appalled.

"Sorry, bad choice of words. Get one of the team to check all suicides by young Asian girls." Benton made a face as he stood up. "There can't be that many, can there?"

Benton shrugged and made for the door. "Hope it's not a can of worms."

"So do I, Mike. So do I. By the way, have we had any leads with Amalia's ring?"

"None so far."

"Well, maybe Hannah's article will nudge a few memories."

"Let's hope so. By the way does Ms Weybridge know about Nadia Chopra?"

"No – I've held back on going public with this one. Don't want to give the idea that we have a serial killer on the loose." Claudia finished her drink. "But it will be useful to see if she's unearthed anything in her research."

"Right. I'll go and get someone to run a check on deaths and suicides of young Asian girls." He looked at his watch. "Probably be Monday now unless you're paying overtime."

"No chance. Doing anything exciting this weekend?"

Benton's smile lit up his face. "I'm taking Josh to the game – Tottenham are playing QPR at home. What about you?"

Momentarily a cloud passed over her face. "Takeaway, wine and a good book – plus I've got some paperwork to get through."

"Right see you Monday, then."

"You will. Bright and early."

But neither knew how early that was destined to be.

CHAPTER FOURTEEN

Hannah was surprised at the detour they made in Brighton. At one point they drew up outside The Grand.

"I thought you'd booked The Queen's."

"I did." Tom left the engine running, checked something in the boot, then returned to the driver's seat and smiled. "All clear."

Hannah was none the wiser but it felt good to relax and let Tom do the worrying – if there was anything to worry about. He hadn't mentioned the tail they'd picked up, and neither had she. She had seen the car in the passenger mirror she'd pulled down so she could see Elizabeth in the back seat. It had become second nature to her, to be aware and wary.

Then they pulled up outside the Metropole. "What, are we on a mystery tour of Brighton's hotels?"

Tom laughed. "No, I thought better of The Queen's especially after your comment about The Dorchester."

"But I was joking." Hannah felt awful.

"I know, but the Metropole has a suite. They didn't know if they'd have one free earlier and I had to ring back." He smiled. "Perseverance pays off."

They were quickly registered and shown to their rooms. Hannah was surprised when Tom had removed Elizabeth's car seat as well as all the travel paraphernalia from the vehicle. He just smiled at her raised eyebrow and loaded it onto the trolley that the bellboy had brought with him.

The bay window in the large sitting room they were

shown to overlooked the seafront where the pier was already lit up. In the bedroom, a travel cot was ready for Hannah to transfer the sleeping Elizabeth into. She'd only opened her eyes for a moment as they entered the lobby and went straight back to sleep.

"Shall we order some dinner from room service?" Tom flopped into an armchair and perused the menu.

"Sounds good. You choose."

Hannah went into the bathroom to unpack the toiletries and Elizabeth's bits and pieces while Tom phoned through their order. She thought she heard him make another call but by then she'd decided to have a quick shower.

When she came back into the room wearing one of her favourite cotton dresses, she felt refreshed and more relaxed. Tom had opened two small bottles of wine from the mini-fridge.

"Here's to some sunshine and sea air." They clinked glasses.

Hannah look a long sip then asked the question that had been uppermost in her mind all the way down. "What happened to that man, Sherlock, who stood in front of me at the church?" Who took the bullet meant for me was what she didn't say but was implicit in her question.

"I really don't know. He was taken to hospital, obviously, but after that I haven't a clue what happened to him. As you know I went straight back to the States and – "

"Couldn't you find out? You must have some connections?"

"I could ask Claudia Turner."

"I've already asked her. Still, maybe she'd give you a different answer."

"What's that supposed to mean?" Tom looked genuinely surprised.

"Nothing, but you seem to know each other rather well."

"True." Tom finished his drink just as there was a knock on the door and room service arrived with their meal and a bottle of Chablis.

Hannah smiled at the memory it evoked of their first meal together in Jo Allen's. He'd ordered Chablis then and she'd wondered if he was one of the corrupt police officers she heard so much about as he'd paid for everything in cash. Tom caught her smile. "We've come a long way, Hannah, and I'm so very glad we met."

"So am I," she said accepting a glass as she sat down at the dining table in the bay window. The sight of the food made her realise she hadn't eaten for ages.

"Bon appétit." Tom raised his glass to her.

"Thank you." It summed up everything and nothing. But Tom seemed to understand.

The weekend was just what she needed. The hotel spa provided her with some relaxation and pampering while Tom took Elizabeth to the small amusement park. Elizabeth loved the indoor swimming pool. They wandered through The Lanes like any couple taking a holiday and later, on the beach, Elizabeth shrieked with delight when the waves splashed her as she took her first hesitant steps into the sea with Tom and Hannah each holding a hand.

They found a family-friendly restaurant, enjoying the food, wine and each other's company. Elizabeth threw a couple of wobblies but that didn't seem to upset Tom. In fact, Tom acted as though to fatherhood born.

In the evening they ordered from room service after putting Elizabeth to bed. Hannah felt both energised and at peace. Time away with Tom was just the tonic she needed. She was startled out of her reverie by a question she hadn't thought would come up. At least not then.

"What will you tell Elizabeth about her biological father?"

The question seemed to come from nowhere. Hannah stared at him. "Why do you ask?"

"I'd have thought that was obvious. I'm hoping to be a part of both your lives and we have to work out what Elizabeth is told – gradually I know."

For once Hannah loved the sound of that "we". She wasn't alone. She had support. Someone in her life who cared. It had come as a cruel shock that Paul, who had wanted to end Elizabeth's life before it had begun was also part of a conspiracy to kill them both – even if he did shape up in the end and save her life. She wasn't sure what she would tell Elizabeth, or how much, but it wasn't something she had to decide now.

"I wasn't planning on telling her anything until she's old enough to understand." Hannah snuggled up to him on the sofa. "But I'm so glad you want to be with me making those decisions."

* * *

When it was time to leave the hotel, a different car was waiting for them. Tom was obviously taking no chances but what had prompted such precautions? Hannah didn't want to ask.

The journey back to London was bitter-sweet. Hannah was not looking forward to saying goodbye again. But they had cleared the air. The sea breeze had helped with that.

"There's something I have to tell you." Tom changed gear and accelerated past a car and then slipped back into the centre lane.

Hannah had been thinking about how good their love-making had been and turned towards him smiling. "What?"

"About when my wife died."

She felt a frisson of fear and hoped it was unfounded. "I thought you said it was a car accident?"

"Yes it was, but she wasn't alone in the car. Craig, my best friend, was with her."

Hannah remained silent. She had often wondered about Tom's past. He had told her some time ago that he'd changed career after the death of his wife. He'd given up teaching and had joined the police.

"She was leaving me. With him. Their suitcases were in the car, but I only found the letter she had left for me after the police arrived to tell me about the accident."

Hannah didn't know how to reply. A double betrayal and a double loss. She understood both but not to this extent.

"You must have been devastated."

"I was. I thought – mistakenly as it turned out – that we had a special relationship. It's taken me a long time to get over that. She was my first love."

Hannah thought about her own relationships. She had never felt a profound love for a man and neither, she thought, had she inspired such love. Only when she had Elizabeth did she experience the depth of emotions that she had never felt possible. Maybe there was something lacking in her?

Then Hannah wondered about 'first love'. Made it sound like there had been others. She wanted to ask him – again – about his relationship with Claudia but she didn't want to ruin the time they had left together. Tom was going to drop her off in Dulwich and then head off to Heathrow Airport.

Hannah studied Tom's profile. A face that had become more special to her than she previously thought possible.

Tom reached for her hand and smiled. "Just wanted you to know, that's all."

"Thank you."

Tom's mobile rang just as they were unpacking the car outside her house. He looked exasperated. "Sorry I have to take this." Hannah unlocked the front door and deposited her bags before going back to collect Elizabeth.

Tom had his back to her as she approached the car but she distinctly heard him say: "No she doesn't know anything." There was a pause, then, "Of course, I'm certain." He listened a moment longer, then ended the call.

Hannah froze. She had to force herself to carry on

as though she'd heard nothing. There was no reason to assume Tom was referring to her, was there? But she knew without doubt that he was. Elizabeth stared up at her as she undid the straps, her fingers fumbling. She clasped her daughter to her and made her face smile at Tom as he walked round the car to help her with the child seat.

Moments later he had driven off and Hannah wondered if she'd just walked blindly into another trap? Was there an ulterior motive for the weekend away? Had it all been an elaborate charade? And what, if anything, didn't she know?

CHAPTER FIFTEEN

After tucking Elizabeth safely into her cot, Hannah ignored the bags to be unpacked and went into her study. Unusually for a weekend, there were three messages on the answerphone. She pressed play.

"Hi Hannah," – Linda's voice – "hope you're still okay to give your talk to our year elevens on Tuesday afternoon. Will meet you in reception at 2.30. Any problems let me know."

The second message sounded as though the call was being made from a railway station. She could hear the background noise but no voice. She pressed delete.

The voice on the third was one she'd least expected to hear: Judy Burton.

"Hi Hannah, I know I'm the last person you want to hear from, but I heard on the grapevine that someone is trying to dig the dirt on you. Not sure why. Sounded serious. Take care."

Well that was guaranteed to make her sleep easier. Was Judy just being her usual spiteful self? Trying to unsettle her? If that was the case she'd succeeded.

Hannah dialled up the Internet and checked her emails. Nothing. She checked everything on her desk. Everything seemed to be how she'd left it. Should she contact Graham? Mr Special Effects as Tom called him. Then those words she'd overheard Tom saying came back to her. "She doesn't know anything." If she couldn't trust Tom, could she – or more importantly should she – rely on Graham?

She went downstairs, not switching on any lights until she'd made sure every door and window was securely locked and she'd drawn all the curtains. Nothing as far as she could see was out of place. But would she know if someone specially trained had searched for she didn't know what without leaving a trace?

Maybe this was just her overactive imagination being set off by Judy's message. But that didn't detract from what she had overheard Tom saying. She sat down on the chair in Elizabeth's room and practiced the breathing exercises the doctor had given her. Her daughter stirred, blissfully unaware of her mother's state of mind.

Hannah crept out. In the kitchen she poured herself a large glass of water and drank slowly, going over in her mind the conversations she'd had with Tom. She couldn't think of anything he'd said or asked that should have alerted her. Sighing, she picked up the copy of *Birdsong* she'd bought in Brighton and decided to have an early night. Sebastian Faulks could be her bedfellow. He, at least, wanted nothing from her but her attention to his narrative.

The telephone beside Claudia Turner's bed rang and she cursed as she made a grab for the handset. As she did so she saw the time on the clock radio: 12.09.

"Turner."

"Ma'am," it was the duty sergeant at the station, "there's been another body found. Peckham Park again."

"Jesus! How long ago?"

"The call came in at 23.45. Uniform are there securing the area. DS Benton is on his way to collect you, Ma'am."

"Okay, thank you, Sergeant."

Claudia was practiced at dressing at a moment's notice and was ready when Mike Benton rang her bell. He took in her jeans, trainers and fleecy jacket and smiled. Not her normal working gear. But he did wonder if she slept in her make-up to be ready so quickly.

She strapped herself into the seat as Benton put the car into gear and drove off. No need for flashing lights; the streets were empty.

"When I said see you Monday, I didn't mean this early," she said in an attempt at a joke. "What have we got, do you know?"

"Young female. And not long dead by the sound of it. We've got all patrols in the area on the lookout." Benton pulled into the car park. "She was found by a couple taking a shortcut home so they may have disturbed the perpetrators. Stopped them hiding the body."

"Right, let's see what we have then." Claudia nodded to the Medical Officer and they set off together.

Another young Asian girl. Why this sudden spate of murders in such a specific age-range and ethnicity? Claudia was at a loss. This girl looked about seventeen. She had been stabbed repeatedly in what looked like a frenzied attack. A different MO. What a start to the week – another family's despair.

CHAPTER SIXTEEN

Hannah's finger hovered over the send icon. She fervently hoped that her article about the suspected murder of Amalia Kumar would help her aunt and perhaps give the police some new leads. So far, according to Claudia Turner, the ring Amalia was assumed to have been wearing before her death had not turned up at any of the Peckham pawnbrokers. The police had contacted other stations in the south-east and sent the details. But nothing had come of it.

She had checked what Sunita and the family would be happy with and had been given carte blanche.

"I want you to write this in the best way you see fit." Sunita sounded frighteningly calm. "Do not worry about our feelings. See if you can stir any memories. Touch a guilty nerve. I have every confidence in you."

Privately Hannah wondered if she should be so trusting. Would she be? She made a note on the email that she wanted to check the subbed copy. The story was sensational enough without adding to it as *The News* subs were prone to do.

The story concentrated on how the perpetrators had tried to make Amalia's death look like suicide. Hannah had highlighted the student's achievements and the total lack of any evidence to suggest she would have taken her own life. Motive for murder was also an enigma.

She pressed send and would await Rory's reaction. In the meantime she had another dilemma that would not, it seemed, go away.

**

The visiting order was the third she had received. Paul Montague was nothing if not persistent. Stubborn was another word she might have used. She really didn't want to see him. Then it occurred to her that she had a get-out clause. She rang the solicitor at *The News*.

Larry Jefferson answered on the third ring. "How can I help you?" he asked when she introduced herself.

His manner towards her had undergone a transformation since their first dealings – he'd been so nasty and officious when *The News* spiked her story about Caroline. After she had been given a contract and, it seemed, Lord Gyles's personal protection, he was actually solicitous. A solicitous solicitor. Hannah smiled at her own joke.

"I just wanted to check something out with you regarding Paul Montague." Did she imagine a pause?

"Fire away."

"Well, he's sent me several visiting orders and, as you know, he's on remand for the part he played in... in ..."

The lawyer spared her the description. "Quite. And as you will be a witness for the prosecution at his trial it would be unethical for you to have any contact with him."

Hannah let out the breath she hadn't realised she was holding. "Thank you. That's exactly what I wanted to hear."

"In fact, I'll contact the governor at the prison and let him know. And Montague's solicitor. Anything else I can help you with?"

"No that's very kind of you. Thank you."

She hung up and tore the visiting order into shreds. If only everything could be sorted so easily.

Shortly afterwards Rory rang to say that her Amalia story was going in the next day.

"You flagged up that you wanted to see the subbed copy?"

"Yes, I hope that's not a problem?"

"Not at all. I'm just checking that you'll be at your desk ready and waiting."

Hannah laughed. "By the way did you enjoy the match?"

"Well a three-all draw was better than defeat. How was your weekend?"

"Interesting. Tom turned up and we went to Brighton."

There was a silence at the other end of the line.

"Rory, are you still there?"

"Yes, sorry Hannah, someone just put something on my desk that I need to deal with. I'll get Angie to call you when the copy's ready to be emailed to you. We'll fax over the layout as well."

Hannah didn't have a chance to thank him before he rang off.

CHAPTER SEVENTEEN

The pupils were already assembled in the classroom they were using for Hannah's talk when she arrived. She'd agonised over what to wear. What image did she want to present? The smart casual of a successful career woman she decided and chose a dress and jacket to fit the part. To celebrate her new contract and increased fee, she'd bought herself some new clothes. Her work outfits hung in her wardrobe, colour-coordinated and at the ready. An absolute luxury – and a time-saver.

Now she scanned the faces as they looked towards her expectantly. A range of skin tones from English rose white to deep ebony. Seeing the African-looking girl reminded Hannah of Mia and the girls who had been trafficked. Those nightmares remained in her memory like an ill-digested meal. She wondered which of the Asian pupils was the one who was always having time off. Or maybe – inevitably – she was absent.

Linda held up her hands, waited for silence and began her introduction. Hannah heard "investigative journalist … exposés … human interest stories", words breaching the electrifying shock she experienced when she looked across to the row of teachers who stood along the back.

They looked friendly enough. Except for one man. Dark hair, clean-shaven, wearing heavy, black-rimmed glasses and a sports jacket that looked as though it had been bought from a charity shop. It didn't suit him. As soon as he saw her looking at him he bent forward and said something to the pupil in front of him. From then on, he seemed to always have a hand, book, something or other obscuring his face. But once or twice during her talk, she caught him staring at her and there was something about him that seemed familiar.

Hannah finished her prepared spiel and Linda asked if there were any questions.

Hands shot up. Linda pointed to a boy in the fourth row. "Michael."

"Do you earn a lot of money?" A few sniggers.

"That depends," Hannah parried. "Regional – local newspapers – and some magazines don't pay very much. You can earn more money working for national newspapers but if you're freelance, like me, there are times when work is scarce."

"You're not very glamorous are you?" It wasn't a question but a statement from a pupil who looked as though she spent every waking moment working on her appearance.

"Look who's talking," shouted one of the boys from the back and she saw the dark-haired teacher bend forward and say something to him. The boy just grinned.

Hannah laughed. "Luckily for me, glamour isn't one of the qualifications you need to be a journalist."

"What qualifications do you need?" Linda had interceded with a question.

Hannah paused, aware she should be pushing formal education. "Apart from A levels or a degree, an open mind, an ability to listen, a good grasp of English language…"

She was interrupted by a boy sitting towards the back.

"Why'd you have to stand outside people's houses and shout at them?"

"What would you know about that, Jimbo? What's your dad been up to?"

The boy ignored the laughter. "I've seen it on the telly, haven't I."

Hannah smiled. "Fortunately I've never had to do that, but sometimes it's necessary if you need to get to the bottom of a story and if someone's been lying or covering up a crime." Hannah hadn't expected to be put on the spot like this.

"My dad says you wrote a good story about girls being smuggled into the country." This came from a girl in the front row who, Hannah noticed, was taking notes.

"Thank you." Hannah looked across at Linda for guidance, not sure about how much to say. "That was a very difficult investigation."

"How did you feel when you found your friend dead in that church in Waterloo?" The question came from a pupil in the middle row of girls.

You could hear the proverbial pin drop. Linda looked as though she was going to say something, but Hannah felt these kids deserved an honest response.

"It was horrendous." She paused. For a moment she was back in the crypt. Her friend's dead body in front of her. "I felt sick. To be honest – I was sick. It was one of the worst experiences of my life."

"I was sick when I found my sister dead. She'd drunk bleach and..." the Asian girl who had been speaking stood up. Her chair clattered back and Hannah wasn't sure whether she was going to pass out or...

The scream reverberated around the room. Several members of staff moved at once towards a white girl who had been sitting next to the Asian one. There seemed no reason for the scream and the girl was lead out of the classroom.

A bell rang. Linda wound up the session. The pupils clapped and then they were gone.

"Sorry about that performance at the end." Linda said no more and Hannah had renewed admiration for teachers and the work they did. They certainly had their work cut out for them at this school. As they were walking back to the reception area, Hannah asked about the male teacher who'd seemed familiar.

"That's Mike Jones. He's a supply. Booked to cover a maternity leave. Oh, there he is. What did you think of the talk, Mike?"

"We could have done without the histrionics."

Hannah could see he would have avoided going over to them, if he could have. She searched for something in her bag but watched the way he walked towards them. The walk. She knew that walk. And he held his left arm awkwardly.

Hannah smiled at him as they shook hands.

"I have the feeling that we've met somewhere before."

"No, I think I would remember." He smiled and pushed his glasses further up his nose. For a moment his eyes stared into hers. "Nice talk. Perhaps some of them will concentrate on their exams if they think they could join you."

"I wouldn't know. Be good to think so." She turned

to Linda and kissed her cheek. "Looks like my cab has arrived. See you soon?"

Mike Jones held the glass door open for her. "Take care."

They were inches apart. And she knew. Her body remembered the way he had pushed her and stood there. Taking a bullet for her on the steps of St John the Evangelist, seconds before Tom had arrived.

"Thank you," she said and walked swiftly to the awaiting car, wondering what the hell he was doing as a supply teacher. Unless, of course, he had been given a medical discharge and this was a new career. Somehow she thought not. She felt sure the man who had been Sherlock, living among the homeless in Cardboard City, was on another undercover mission. But in a school? Linda's school?

When she returned home there was a message on the answerphone. Sunita Kumar's distinctive tones greeted her. "Hannah. We have read the article. Thank you."

CHAPTER EIGHTEEN

Sasha admired the ring on her finger, twisting her hand to examine it from all angles. It was by far the most beautiful piece of jewellery she had ever owned. The fact that it had been given to her by Ahmed made it even more special. He had been so excited when he presented it to her.

"I know it isn't new but when I saw it in the shop window, I knew it was perfect for you."

He kissed the top of her head and caressed her bump.

"It's lovely. But you shouldn't spend money on me. Not now."

Ahmed's face darkened. "I can do what I like for my wife. I want you always to have beautiful things." He couldn't see the irony of the words, which were spoken in their pokey one-bedroomed flat with its tiny kitchen and bathroom. They were on the council list but it could take ages for them to be rehoused.

Sasha pulled him down on to the sofa beside her. "Thank you. I love it." She kissed him out of his bad mood.

Now she looked at the ring with a heavy heart. Her mum had read in the newspaper that a similar ring had been missing from a girl found drowned in Peckham Park. Sasha knew it wasn't just similar. She had read the inscription *For Amalia all my love Sunita*. She knew the jewellery shop where Ahmed said he had bought it was also a pawnbroker. She had thought someone down on their luck had had to sell it. That is if Ahmed had actually bought it. Maybe he had found it. Either way she would have to hand it over to the police. And Ahmed would be furious with her.

She hauled herself up off the sofa, put the ring into a zipped pocket in her bag and locked the door behind her when she left. The rest of the house, divided into flats, was quiet. Unusually so for this time of day.

As she made her way down the stairs, her heel caught in the threadbare carpet on a stair and she went flying forwards. She tried to stop herself, terrified for her baby, but landed in a heap, hitting her head on the tiled floor.

CHAPTER NINETEEN

Hannah was curious to see a teenage girl standing outside her front door. She was in school uniform, with her satchel hooked over one shoulder. Her hair had a luminous black sheen and was neatly braided. She appeared relieved at seeing Hannah who wondered how long she'd been waiting there.

"Hello. Can I help you?" She pulled the keys out of her pocket and the girl moved aside for her as she unlocked the door.

"You came to give a talk at my school. On Tuesday this week," the girl said without preamble.

"Yes?" Hannah switched off the alarm placed just inside the door.

"Well, you're a journalist and you write about people's difficult situations."

"Sometimes I do, yes."

"I need your help."

Hannah's throat tightened as she remembered the last young woman who turned up on her doorstep. Caroline – the prostitute known as Princess – was never far from her thoughts. That she had not been able to prevent her death weighed heavily in her heart. She had let her down. At least this girl wasn't badly beaten up, and it wasn't the middle of the night but a bright, spring afternoon. Janet was out at the baby gym with Elizabeth, so she invited the girl in, wondering if she really should have told her she'd meet her somewhere else. A public place?

"So –?" Hannah directed her into the sitting room with a gesture.

"Alison." The look on Hannah's face must have betrayed her thought. "My name is Alesha Kaur but I use Alison sometimes – it helps with forms and things."

Hannah nodded feeling more uncomfortable.

"Alesha is such a pretty name."

The girl smiled and sat down on the sofa.

"Can I get you anything?"

"No, I'm fine thank you."

"So why have you come to see me Alesha, and how did you get my address?"

"Oh that was easy – I asked at the school office. Said I wanted to send a thank-you note and the temp working there gave it to me."

Hannah tried not to let her annoyance show as she scratched her left hand. She'd had to fill in a form at reception before being allowed to enter the school. As she'd waived her speaker's fee, she'd assumed the school hadn't kept those details and certainly wouldn't give them out to pupils. She would phone the school later. And ask Linda. It was a terrible lapse of confidentiality. Although under ordinary circumstances, she supposed it wasn't.

"I see. And you are here because –"

"My cousin has gone missing. My aunt said she's away visiting family but I'm sure she would have mentioned it. We get on really well. We talk all the time. Surjit is not much older than me. She is to be married soon. It's an arranged marriage. But she seemed happy. No, not happy, resigned to what would happen, I think. I'm worried about her." The words came out in a rush as though the speaker had to say them before they disappeared. The face looking at Hannah was a mixture of anger and anxiety.

"But maybe she's doing exactly what your aunt said and visiting family?"

"I don't know. I think it's more than that. There have been arguments. And I've heard my parents talking…"

"Have you asked them outright?"

"Yes, but they change the subject. My aunt is a very difficult woman. Miss Weybridge, I'm scared for Surjit. I have written all her details down for you." She handed Hannah an envelope just as the doorbell rang. Alesha grabbed her hand. "Please help me find her."

Hannah looked at the portable video monitor on the table beside her. An irate-looking bearded man wearing a turban was pushing the bell again. "Do you know this man?"

Alesha looked over Hannah's shoulder and nodded, her dark eyes widened in fear.

Hannah went and opened the door but before she could say anything the man had pushed past her, shouting, "Where is she? Where is my daughter?"

Uninvited he went straight into the sitting room. "Dad?" Alesha moved towards her father.

Hannah realised that what she had thought of as fear was surprise. Alesha was surprised but she clearly wasn't afraid at seeing him.

He, on the other hand, was furious. "What is she doing here?" He rounded on Hannah. "What is she saying to you?"

Hannah had seconds to absorb the situation. "You must be Alesha's father." She smiled in what she hoped was a placatory manner. "You must be so proud of her. My name is Hannah Weybridge and I met Alesha at her school when I was giving a talk. One of her teachers, Linda Brown, knew I was looking for an occasional babysitter and recommended your daughter. We were just having a chat about it."

"Is this true?" The man had lost some of his bluster. "Daughter, are you trying to find work as a babysitter?"

The girl looked mortified and nodded. "I can earn some money and still do my school work."

Hannah had swiftly pushed the envelope Alesha had given her out of sight.

"Perhaps you could leave me your telephone number, Alesha. Here's my card with mine on. If that's okay with you, Mr Kaur?"

"Mr Singh. My name is Mr Singh – Kaur is for the women."

"I apologise."

"It doesn't matter. If you two have finished, I'll take my daughter home now." He was already pushing Alesha out of the room.

"Of course." Hannah smiled at the girl.

"And if you do want her to babysit you should arrange it through her mother or me and I will bring her and collect her." He had snatched Hannah's card from his daughter's hand. "Our number is 081 777 7878."

Hannah scribbled it down on a scrap of paper. "Thank you, Mr Singh."

In the hall Hannah managed to slip another card into

the girl's hand. Alesha secreted it into her pocket.

"Thank you, Miss Weybridge." Alesha, she realised, had visibly relaxed after her lie about babysitting and from that moment didn't look at all intimidated by her father. His bluster had all been for her benefit.

As she shut the door behind them, Hannah wondered if the father always followed his daughter like that. She went back into the sitting room and retrieved the envelope.

Inside was a photo of a pretty girl in a turquoise sari. On a sheet of paper in precise handwriting were Surjit's date of birth, full name, address and the shop where she worked. Alesha had also written a note to Hannah asking her to contact her via a friend's address but said she would phone her when she could, assuming Hannah had given her the number. Hannah smiled. The girl seemed to have covered all bases.

The name of Surjit's workplace rang a bell. It was a fabric shop in Peckham. Hannah had been in there once looking for a particular silk she wanted to make a dress. That was a while ago. She never had the time for dressmaking now. But she still had a fabric remnant somewhere. She could use that.

Hannah's mobile rang. Unusual during the evening. Claudia Turner sounded a little breathless.

"Is your TV on? Switch on *Crimewatch*. We've got a slot at the end of the programme. Only just heard. It's their one hundredth anniversary edition so a bit of a coup really. They're going to show pictures of Amalia Kumar's ring..."

"That's brilliant, Claudia. Does her family know?"

"Yes, we contacted them and we have an officer sitting with them just in case anyone rings."

"Right thanks for letting me know."

"Let's hope it generates some useful leads. Good article by the way." And with that Claudia rang off.

Hannah switched on the TV. It was ten-twenty and the programme presenters Sue Cook and Nick Ross were asking the public if anyone knew anything about the murder of a fifty-six-year-old man who had been found in East London in February.

What a long time to wait to find out this man's identity. And then, there it was, the photograph of Amalia's ring as well as a photograph of the girl herself who "had drowned in suspicious circumstances in Peckham Rye park". Viewers were invited to phone the studio on a free dedicated number if they had any information about any of the crimes featured in the programme. The Crimewatch Update would be on at 11.50pm. Hannah wondered if she should stay up to watch it but suspected she'd know soon enough if there were any promising leads. Let the police do their job.

CHAPTER TWENTY

There was a buzz in the office the following day that had nothing to do with it being a Friday and the thirteenth. Seeing the photographs of Amalia and her ring on the television had reminded people of the information telephone number the newspaper ran under Hannah's story on Amalia Kumar, which had now received quite a few calls. Many of them anonymous. Some trying to sell info. One of the secretaries had been given the tedious task of transcribing them all.

"But you never know," Rory said as he sipped his coffee and sat on the corner of Hannah's desk, "there might just be a golden nugget in all that shit."

"Let's hope so. The ring has such sentimental value for the aunt and could lead to Amalia's killer or killers."

"Be good to get a witness or two…" Rory wandered back to his desk and its usual clutter. He was supervising the team working on the follow up to the major political story – the death of Labour leader John Smith the day before after he had suffered the second of two massive heart attacks. Colleagues were describing him as "the best Prime Minister Britain never had" and most of the cuttings had mentioned his chosen luxury on *Desert Island Discs* – a crate of champagne.

Hannah made a note to remind herself to phone Joe that evening then straightened the papers Rory had moved when he'd perched on her desk.

She looked up when Rory slammed down his phone and came over to her looking grim.

"George wants to see you in her office."

"And you've been delegated to escort me because...?" Hannah smiled up at him but the look of concern on his face brought a blush to her face in contrast to the chill she felt. Picking up her handbag, she walked through the gap between desks feeling that everyone was staring at her which most probably wasn't true as they all had deadlines to meet. A mere glance was all she merited these days now that Judy wasn't there to stoke the animosity.

Rory tapped on the editor's door, stood aside and followed Hannah in. She was stunned to see the solicitor there. She immediately wondered if she'd breached her contract in some way and they were going to dispense with her services. However Georgina Henderson's demeanour seemed reassuring. She indicated the sofa next to the armchair she was sitting in and nodded to the lawyer as Hannah sat down with Rory next to her.

"Larry has something to tell you. I am really sorry but it's upsetting and seemingly totally unexpected."

He cleared his throat. "Hannah, we had a telephone conversation a few days ago." It sounded like a question but was a fact.

"Ye-es."

"As you know I said I would be in contact with Paul Montague's solicitor and the prison governor."

Hannah nodded. Whatever it was, why didn't he just get to the point?

"The governor contacted me today." He swallowed hard and she was mesmerised the rise and fall of his Adam's apple. "I'm very sorry to have to tell you that

Mr Montague was found dead in his cell this morning. It appears he took his own life." He looked down at his hands and then up into her face. "I'm very sorry, Hannah."

The room was silent. She could hear her pulse beating in her ear. She felt sick. Her face was wet. The tears had leaked out silently. She hadn't realised she was crying, but as she did so she felt her temperature rise.

"Here, drink this." The editor handed her a glass of water.

"Think she needs something a bit stronger," Rory said, but was ignored.

"We'll get a car to take you home, Hannah. If there's anything we can do?" Georgina let the question hang between them. It was her dismissal.

Hannah had no recollection of leaving the building. The car was waiting for her outside. Not one of the usual ones, Rory noticed. George's chauffeur was at the wheel.

"Is anyone at home? Do you want me to call someone?"

Hannah shook her head. "It's my fault. All my fault."

"You are not responsible for Paul's actions, Hannah. None of them."

She gripped his hand. "Thanks, Rory. It's just such a shock."

He nodded. "I'll call you later." He stood back and the car glided away.

By the time Hannah was at home, ensconced in her study, she had calmed down and was embarrassed by her outburst of grief. She wasn't sure what to do next. Paul's parents were dead and she didn't know anything about his brother or other family members. Presumably, the prison authorities would sort out all the formalities. And there would be an inquest. She wondered if she would be called to it. She had no idea how inquests were conducted. And then there was the question of Elizabeth. Paul's name was not on her birth certificate – for that she was truly grateful – so maybe both of them would be out of the picture. She sincerely hoped so. She was saddened by Paul's death. Was the fact that she refused to visit him a factor? Did it push him over the edge? Suicide made the people left behind feel guilty, that they should have or could have done something to prevent it. She was no exception.

She wondered how this would be covered in the press. How had he done it? Hannah looked up the statistics for prison suicide – mostly single figures each year – and saw most killed themselves by hanging. Hannah managed to get to the bathroom just in time to bring up the bile, which had threatened ever since she'd heard the news.

She was just rinsing her mouth when the telephone rang. She let it go through to the answerphone and listened to a voice she'd never heard before: Paul Montague's solicitor, Neville Rogers. Hannah picked up the phone.

"Hello, Hannah Weybridge here."

"Ah, Ms Weybridge, I was just about to ask you to call me as soon as you could. As Paul Montague's solicitor, I am very sorry to have to inform you that I've learned from the prison governor that Mr Montague died this morning."

"Yes, I heard."

"Really?" He paused. "The press hounds are quick off the mark."

There was no answer to that. She assumed he knew where she worked.

"Anyway, Mr Montague left instructions with me that in the event of his death…"

"What? Did he plan it? Did he plan to kill himself?" Hannah's voice had risen an octave.

"As far as I am aware, that was not his intention."

"So why…"

Neville Rogers cleared his throat loudly. "There will be an inquest. But these cases are usually a formality. I can say that I never had the impression that Mr Montague would take his own life, but I do know he was devastated by the situation he found himself in. Especially in relation to you and his daughter."

Hannah could feel her anger rising like a tide of coruscating acid. "A daughter he had never wanted or had anything to do with until… until…" Hannah swallowed the sob.

"That is as may be. However I do have some paperwork for you to see so perhaps we could arrange a mutually convenient time to visit my office?"

"You're rather quick off the mark, aren't you?"

"I am just following instructions, Ms Weybridge."

Hannah agreed to go to his office on Monday morning.

"My deepest condolences," he said as he rang off.

Hannah was furious. The man had made her feelings seem insignificant. Still she supposed this was the last work he would be doing for Paul, who had saved the taxpayer an immense amount of money by avoiding a criminal trial. If only she had responded to his letter. Explained why she couldn't visit him. Maybe if she hadn't pushed him away... Her mind went back to the good times they'd had. It was like a film playing in slow motion in her head. Their life together such as it was. The fun. There had been a time when she thought they would carry on forever in their semi-detached way. Then Hannah had become pregnant and everything changed. Paul hadn't exactly broken her heart but he had dented it.

When the doorbell rang Hannah was surprised to see a motorbike courier standing outside. She opened the door and he handed her an envelope that she had to sign for. Hannah didn't recognise the handwriting. As she walked upstairs to her study, she turned it over and over again in her hand. Why would anyone send a letter by courier rather than phone or email? She sat at her desk, took a deep breath and opened the envelope. The letter was handwritten on HMPS notepaper.

Dear Ms Weybridge,

Please excuse this intrusion, especially at what is no doubt a difficult time for you.

I am the Chaplain at Brixton prison and during his time here Paul Montague came to see me regularly and attended services. This may surprise you. Paul told me that he had never previously been interested in religion. Loss of liberty affects people in all sorts of different ways.

Paul talked to me about what he had done; his feelings and hopes. Obviously that was all confidential but what I can say is that at no time did he give me the impression he would take his own life...

Hannah stared out of the window seeing nothing. Why had the chaplain contacted her? Clearly Paul had mentioned her and, presumably, given him her address. She wondered what he and Paul had discussed. Did this chaplain know more than he was letting on about Paul's suicide? Prison must have affected him profoundly for him to have killed himself. There had been a good chance he would get a relatively light sentence as he had pleaded guilty and it had been his swift action that had saved Elizabeth and Janet. So why had he taken his own life?

There were some contact details on the letter. The Reverend Martyn Jones had given her his home number. Should she phone him? Hear what he had to say? Interesting that a priest and Paul's lawyer had made a point of contacting her.

She rang the number but the call went through to the chaplain's paging service. She left her name and number and tried to concentrate on the cuttings she had on missing Asian girls. There were not that many and most of them were short pieces reported in local papers. No one ever seemed to follow up the disappearances.

When the telephone ringing broke into her thoughts, she was grateful for the interruption. She thought it would be the chaplain returning her call but was surprised to hear the voice of the pathologist, Dr Matthew Carter.

"Hannah, I've got something that should help you."

"Yes?"

"I kept thinking about Amalia Kumar and how she died. It just didn't add up. Self-preservation would have made her fight for breath ... Anyway, I ran a toxicology test and found a high level of diazepam in her blood. She was drugged before drowning."

Hannah silently absorbed his words.

"I'm sorry, I should have thought of that before."

"Thank you, Dr Carter. That does make more sense now. Could you email the findings and I'll pass them on to the police?"

Hannah connected to the Internet in anticipation. There was an email from Tom. *Hi, wonderful to be with you and Elizabeth last weekend. More anon. Love Tom.* So brief she wondered why he had bothered. It unsettled her remembering the conversation she'd overheard. Had the weekend just been a ploy to check out whatever it was she was supposed not to know? Should she tell him about Paul? Especially as he had asked her what she would tell Elizabeth about him. She decided against it. Everything had changed now. She'd avoid the platitudes for as long as she could.

She forwarded the email which arrived from Dr Carter to DI Turner.

Claudia rang her about an hour later. "Thanks for that info from the pathologist. How are you?"

"I assume you're referring to Paul Montague's death?"

If Claudia was surprised by Hannah's abrupt tone, she didn't react. "Yes, that must have come as a shock."

"To be honest I just feel rather numb."

"Yes well," Claudia sounded embarrassed. "Let's have that drink sometime soon. I'll call you next week. By the way, we haven't had any leads on Amalia's ring. If we do I'll keep you posted." And with that she hung up.

Hannah looked at her watch and realised that Janet would be needing to leave. She went downstairs and found her giving Elizabeth her tea. She smiled as the child held out her sticky hands. "Mama." She beamed.

"There's something I have to tell you Janet, and there's no easy way." She sat down at the table with her daughter and Janet. "Paul died this morning. Apparently he killed himself."

Janet's face turned crimson, then paled. "Oh no how awful." She refrained from making any further comment. Hannah supposed this was in deference to her as she'd always been so tetchy on the subject of Elizabeth's father.

"Anyway, I wanted to tell you just in case it comes up on the news somewhere."

"Thanks. Is it okay if I shoot off now?"

"Of course." Hannah's smile was weak and weary. "See you tomorrow evening for babysitting?"

"Yes." Janet looked as though she wanted to say more but decided against it and quickly left the house.

With Janet gone, Hannah hugged her daughter to her and wept.

CHAPTER TWENTY-ONE

Elizabeth struggled as Hannah strapped her into the buggy. "Walk Mama, walk," came the imperious directive. No way, thought Hannah, not on a Saturday morning in Peckham. She squatted so their faces were level with each other and caressed her daughter's cheek. She searched the face for similarities to Paul. Yes, there was something about the frown and the shape of her head. Hannah remembered that when she was born Elizabeth had looked the image of her father – as far as newborns can look like adults of the opposite sex in their thirties. That had gradually faded. She certainly looked like photos of herself as a toddler. She felt awful that she hadn't wanted Paul in their lives and now he was gone forever. She'd assumed that Elizabeth might want to contact her father when she was older – now she would never have the opportunity of doing so or of knowing him.

"We're going shopping and they'll be lots of people about." That's what Hannah needed. People she didn't know filling the empty spaces.

"Shops!" Elizabeth beamed. She associated shops with being given treats and made a fuss of.

"Yes, and it's a lovely day so maybe we'll go to the park this afternoon."

Elizabeth clapped her hands. "Ducks," she said. "Swings."

Locking up the house always took a lot longer now and Hannah was meticulous. Nasty surprises were the last thing she wanted. Her locks were top of the range but had they been secure enough to keep someone out of her house last weekend? Better not to dwell on that thought.

She decided to walk via the bus route into Peckham rather than a stroll through the back streets. Hannah needed to be amongst the shopping crowds.

Rye Lane on a Saturday morning was evidently the place to see and be seen. Hannah was grateful for the buggy, which helped to clear a pathway. As she made her way along the crowded pavement, the odour of raw meat assailed her along with far more appetising smells of spices and herbs, presumably unheard of when this first became a fashionable shopping street a century before. When she had first moved to the area, Hannah had loved shopping in Jones & Higgins, the prestigious department store which had closed down some years before. Its distinctive 1930s building and tower remained at the top end of the Lane like a beacon to a more glamorous past. Now the area, although vibrant, was no longer smart, as evidenced by the copious amounts of litter everywhere.

The shops boasted foods from Africa and Asia and everywhere in between. If you wanted some special ingredient for a recipe, this is where you came. Hannah slowed her pace to keep in step behind the group of Afro-Caribbean women who were strolling in front of her, hips swaying to the rhythm of their conversation and laughter. As they turned to each other she caught sight of their beautiful faces, alight with the joy of just being. Hannah envied them. She couldn't remember the last time she'd laughed out loud with a friend. Even with Elizabeth she felt her isolation keenly, although her daughter did bring her a special joy. She hadn't always been so solitary. As an only child she'd grown up loving her own company, being able to lose herself in a book with no sibling to disturb her. But as she made her way through school and university she found kindred spirits and passing friendships. Recently, however, there were too few disturbances of a joyful kind in her life.

Hannah was jerked from her thoughts when one of the women ahead of her stopped short, threw her head back and bellowed in delight. "Alleluia sister," she said once she regained her breath and the group continued their saunter.

Hannah could feel herself absorbing some of their delight. She had reached the fabric shop and wheeled Elizabeth inside. It was a tight fit, pushing the buggy down the aisles of fabrics of every hue and texture. There was that lovely smell of new textiles along with faint exotic aromas that Hannah couldn't place.

An assistant dressed in a bright orange sari with red and turquoise sequins decorating the edges greeted her with a smile. Hannah noticed the henna designs on her hands and a beautiful manicure.

"Good morning. How can I help you, ma'am?" Her low sing-songy voice was inviting.

Hannah smiled and produced the fragment of silk. "I was wondering if you had anything like this in stock? I bought it here some time ago."

The young woman's hand caressed the fabric. Her whole face radiated her smile. "I think we may still have some in the stockroom. I'll check for you."

Hannah watched her glide along the aisle, unhurried but purposeful. She glanced down at Elizabeth who seemed enchanted by the array of rainbow colours around her. "Aren't these pretty?"

Elizabeth looked up at her. "Pretty. Pretty," she repeated.

A group of teenage girls was huddled around a display of what must be, Hannah thought, a traditional wedding outfit. The mannequin wearing it had an elaborate hairstyle fixed with jewels, her hands were decorated with abstract henna designs and she sported a half-veil across her face. The eyes were dull in comparison to so much finery.

Hannah edged nearer to eavesdrop – a futile action as their excited thoughts were expressed in what she thought was rapid Punjabi. The girls looked at her and giggled. Elizabeth shouted "hello" several times and they waved back to her.

The assistant returned. "I'm so sorry, it seems we have run out of this one. May I show you some others? Very similar."

Hannah nodded and followed her with the buggy. "Is Surjit still working here?" she asked when they were out of earshot of the older woman who seemed to be the owner.

"Surjit? I – "

"Surjit Gupta? My babysitter was telling me that she is brilliant at sewing."

The assistant looked at her through narrowed eyes. "I think you must be mistaken. We have no Surjit working here."

"Oh, I'm sorry, I must have got the name of the shop wrong."

"Yes." The assistant looked away. "This fabric is very similar to the one you had. It comes in a range of colours."

Hannah ran her fingers over the silks. "Which colour do you like, Elizabeth?"

The toddler wasn't listening to her mother; her attention was absorbed by the assistant's hands. The henna, colourful manicure and the rings adorning her fingers were like a magnet.

The assistant knelt down beside her. "Do you like the pictures on my hand? They were done for a friend's wedding."

Elizabeth grabbed a finger. "Pretty." The assistant laughed and smiled up at Hannah.

"She's adorable."

"Thank you. I think so but then I'm biased. I think I'll take three metres of this one, please."

The chosen fabric was lifted down and taken to the measuring table. As she unrolled the material against the ruler fixed on the side, she said so quietly that Hannah almost thought she'd imagined it: "Surjit does work here but she has not been in for some time. We've been told to say nothing."

"Thank you," Hannah said as the assistant folded the cloth. "Do you know where she might have gone?" The girl shook her head. "I'll be sure to come back if I need any more," Hannah said more loudly as she smiled over at the older woman at the back of the shop who had been staring at them. The assistant took Hannah's money and returned with her change.

"Goodbye." She handed over the package

"Bye... bye..." Elizabeth waved enthusiastically from her buggy.

The crowds on the pavement outside the fabric shop seemed to be even more animated. A group of young Rasta men leaned against the window openly smoking joints. Hannah gazed down at her daughter and decided to take the next left turning and walk back home via the residential streets in the hope Elizabeth would nod off in less distracting surroundings.

As she made her way home Hannah wondered about all the secrecy surrounding Surjit's disappearance. Surely a girl going missing would be worrying at the least. A police matter? Or did someone know where she was? Her mother? Had she been spirited away for a reason? The journalist in her wanted to keep digging. Her maternal side thought there could be a good reason and she should leave well alone. Families. Hannah pushed a little faster and smiled down at Elizabeth whose eyes were heavy as she fought off sleep.

CHAPTER TWENTY-TWO

The sound of voices greeted Hannah when David opened the front door. She had been invited to dinner but had assumed it would be just her. She was also slightly late as Janet had had a last-minute problem with her mother. Hannah wondered how she coped, looking after a child during the daytime as well as caring for her mother who was becoming increasingly disabled and dependent on her. What sort of a life was that for a young woman?

To add to her discomfort, it was raining heavily after the morning sunshine and although Linda and David only lived a few minutes' walk away, her footwear and legs were soaked. Hannah hadn't told them about Paul's suicide and had anticipated kicking off her shoes and having a relaxing evening – just the three of them. Judging by the noise level coming from the sitting room, they would be far more in numbers and Hannah felt the familiar coil of anxiety gripping her stomach.

David kissed her cheek and took her raincoat and umbrella. "Come through and have a drink – Linda's in the kitchen just adding the finishing touches…" He steered her away from the direction of the kitchen where Hannah had hoped to sneak off to and into the sitting room. It was a larger house than Hannah's and the furniture had been collected in an ad hoc fashion over their years together giving it a warm and lived in glow. Usually Hannah loved being here.

Silence fell as she entered the room. Hannah smiled.

"Meet Hannah the hack –" David's joke was wearing

thin for the butt of it – "Maria, Rob, Jude, Ben and Mike. Red or white?"

"White, please." Hannah tried not to show how disconcerted she was.

"We met before – at the talk you gave at the school." Mike moved forward and shook her hand. He looked relaxed and not at all put out to see her.

"Of course, nice to see you again." Hannah accepted the glass of white wine and took a large gulp. Mike was on his own. As she was. Surely Linda hadn't set her up? He didn't look at all embarrassed and as he seemed to know Maria and Ben; she assumed they too taught at Kingsville.

Hannah was intrigued that he fitted in so well here. Given that his last haunt was Cardboard City in the Bull Ring. She had always had her suspicions about the mysterious Sherlock. Then he had saved her life by taking the bullet meant for her and she'd never been able to thank him. He had disappeared in an ambulance and any enquiries she made about him had drawn a blank.

Now he looked every inch the part of a supply teacher. Clean-shaven and serious with his heavy rimmed glasses. He pushed them up on to his nose as he stared across at her while he chatted to Ben. He was either a very good actor or she was completely wrong about him.

They were seated next to each other at the dining table. "Think we may have been set up, don't you," he said under cover of refilling her glass. He didn't look at all annoyed whereas Hannah was seething with embarrassment.

Linda came in with the main course – poached salmon

– and managed to avoid looking directly at her, a smile at the ready for all her guests.

"So Hannah, what are you working on now or is it all under wraps?"

Hannah composed her face into what she hoped was a secretive expression. She could almost feel Linda's metaphorical kick on David's shins.

"Oh nothing high profile. I'm hoping Joe Rawlington will start dishing the dirt on his fellow MPs – we were at university together." She poured some more wine into her glass. "Or perhaps we'll start investigating John Major's baby –" there was total silence before she added, "Ofsted" and everyone laughed.

Mercifully the conversation moved on to school inspections, the fall in house prices and lack of nursery places.

"Neat parry there."

She turned. Mike was smiling at her. "So what do you do when you're not exposing the peccadillos of the governing classes?"

"I'm a mother. Not much time for anything else."

He looked surprised. "Boy or girl?"

"Girl. Elizabeth." He didn't register any recognition. Had she got this totally wrong? Maybe he was who he said he was. Sherlock was just an uncanny resemblance.

"So why a supply teacher?" She really wanted to ask, "Are you Sherlock?" But she thought she would sound ridiculous. She was waiting for him to give her the clues she needed.

He smiled and pushed his glasses up his nose again. "I like to travel and like this I'm not committed. It gives me the best of both worlds – a job I love and time for other things."

Hannah wondered how he financed his travels but didn't like to ask. She was horrified when Jude addressed her from across the table, "Aren't you the journalist who discovered her friend murdered in that big church in Waterloo?"

There was an awkward silence; all eyes on Hannah. She swallowed a large gulp of wine. "Yes I am."

"So you also wrote the article about trafficked Somali girls?" Hannah nodded. Jude raised her glass to her. "Thank you. That exposé was very powerful to read and you saved a number of girls, or so I heard."

"Jude works in social services," Linda said.

"For my sins." She smiled. "Anyway, good on you."

Rob looked across at her. "I read your piece on the poor girl who drowned in Peckham Park. Good thing the family got that second post mortem done."

"Yes it was." Hannah was relieved that no one reading her article would have known how involved she'd been in advising the aunt.

"Dessert?" Linda stood up and cleared the plates. To Hannah's surprise, Mike stood and took them from her while she picked up the serving dishes.

Wine, good food and interesting company diverted Hannah's thoughts from Paul and why he had killed himself. She was thankful now that she hadn't told Linda and David. It had been an age since she'd been invited to a proper dinner party. No one, it seemed, wanted an extra woman at their table. She could almost forgive Linda for inviting Mike. Almost.

***

As they were moving on to more comfortable seats, Jude said, "I hope I didn't embarrass you earlier. I can't begin to imagine what it must have been like to discover your friend's death like that."

They sat down next to each other on a sofa. "Linda mentioned that you might be looking into Asian girls going missing. I might be able to help." She gave Hannah her card then joined in the general conversation which had moved on to what would happen in the Labour party leadership.

Just as Hannah was leaving, Mike offered to walk her home.

"It's only round the corner, not far at all." Hannah tried to dissuade him.

"Then it won't take me out of my way."

They said goodbye to their hosts. Hannah was surprised to see him unlock a bike from the side gate but made no comment. She wondered what he would say now they were on their own but he remained silent until they reached her door. She could sense he was eyeing up her security arrangements.

He waited for her to unlock the door, standing closer than Hannah felt comfortable with.

"Thank you for walking me home. Goodnight."

Mike leaned towards her and for one awful moment she thought he was going to kiss her. Instead he said so quietly she almost didn't catch his words, "It wasn't suicide." Hannah stared at him. "Paul Montague didn't kill himself." And then he was on his bike and speeding away.

CHAPTER TWENTY-THREE

Hannah had spent most of the night with Mike's words going round and round in her head. "It wasn't suicide. Paul Montague didn't kill himself." And, of course, the big question: how did he know? And what did he know?

Should she contact him? Linda presumably had a telephone number for him. Eventually she fell into a disturbed sleep. In the morning she couldn't remember her dreams but the dread they had caused remained like a storm cloud hovering above her. Damn Mike Smith – Sherlock – or whoever he was.

She phoned Linda who teased her when she asked for Mike's number after thanking her for dinner.

"My little ploy worked then?"

"No, there's something he mentioned that I want to ask him about."

"Oh yes..." Linda didn't sound convinced. "Anyway sorry to disappoint you but I don't have his number. I invited him at school. But I'll ask him for it tomorrow."

Hannah had to be satisfied with that. And tomorrow she'd also contact DI Claudia Turner to see if she had any information.

"We all have our secrets, as you well know." Lady Celia Rayman was replying to Hannah's comment that she thought Sunita Kumar was holding something back from her. Celia smiled at Mary who was dressing a doll with Elizabeth on the settee.

Hannah sipped her coffee. She and Elizabeth had been

invited for Sunday lunch. Mary had prepared a delicious roast with an array of tempting dishes for Elizabeth to try. And the toddler was determined to charm her hosts. Fortunately she'd slept in the cab on the way over so she was on her best behaviour.

They were in the room Hannah had visited so many times before. A room that had borne witness to confessions and revelations. But there was a difference now. The furniture was all the same, as was the layout. But there was a subtle change in the atmosphere that Hannah hadn't expected. A lightness. A huge portrait of Liz that had been completed by an artist using photographs, hung above the mantelpiece. It was astonishing and captivated Liz in all her beauty and complexity. Hannah found her attention drawn to it time and again.

"How did you first meet Sunita, Celia?"

Lady Rayman considered this. "About ten years ago, I think, wasn't it Mary?"

Mary looked up, her hand resting on Elizabeth's shoulder. "Yes I think so. Some fundraising event you went to at the Indian embassy. She was there with her brother."

"That's right. It was after those appalling floods and landslides which wiped out several villages and they were raising money for the survivors. There was an auction."

"Yes we donated one of the Turner sketches– a minor work but the name sold it. Always hated the thing myself." Mary's attention went back to Elizabeth and doll-dressing.

Celia looked thoughtful. "There was something about her. Sunita. A sadness. No, maybe not sadness exactly but a sense of resignation. Anyway who are we to talk?"

"The loss of her niece has hit her particularly hard. She was vehement that she hadn't committed suicide. And it seems she was right, of course."

"They were very close. Lovely girl. Brought her here once or twice."

"They were so alike," Mary said, almost to herself. "It was as though Sunita poured all her maternal instincts into the child."

"I wonder why she didn't marry?" Hannah said charmed by the image of Mary and Elizabeth playing together. It made her think of her own parents and what they were missing.

"Her fiancé was killed. Then she came to England. Maybe she just didn't meet anyone to mend her heart."

"So how long ago was this?"

Celia looked at Hannah, her expression unreadable. "I really don't know. You'll have to ask her if you think it's important. But tread lightly, dear. We know we can trust you but Sunita doesn't know why or our story. She may have her own reasons for being circumspect."

Elizabeth trotted over and stood imperiously in front of Celia. "CC–" the child's attempt at Lady Rayman's name. "Cuddle!" and with that she hoisted herself into the older woman's lap and snuggled into her arms. Celia smiled down at her and in that moment Hannah was reminded of how much Celia had lost. A daughter and an unborn grandchild.

"Now little Miss, shall we see if we can find somewhere cosy for you to have a little nap?"

Elizabeth slid to the floor and took the proffered hand.

"Don't you drop off too, dear," Mary said as they left the room. Celia didn't reply but murmured something and Elizabeth giggled.

Hannah smiled across at Mary. "How are you both?" she asked once the door had closed.

"Taking a day at a time. It's hard but people have been very kind. Liz was a very special person and not just to us. So the charity is our way of coping and paying tribute to her. Keeping her close to us."

Hannah nodded. She had been invited to the launch of The Elizabeth Rayman Trust but was a little peeved that she hadn't been asked to join them as a trustee. Maybe she reminded them of how Liz had died? Or perhaps they didn't see her as trustee material?

"And what about you?" Mary gave her a hug. "Any news from Tom?"

"Yes, in fact he had a meeting in London and tagged on a few days leave so he surprised me last weekend with a trip to Brighton. It was good to get away for a couple of days. Elizabeth loved paddling in the sea."

"And?" There was a look of concern on Mary's face that the younger woman couldn't fathom.

"Whatever he's been working on in New York is due to finish soon and then he should be back in London. We'll have to see what we'll see." Hannah thought about confiding in her about the overheard telephone conversation but decided that would be unfair. She had other, less palatable news to impart.

"Mary – there is something I have to tell you..." Hannah scratched at her hand.

"Just me?" She looked puzzled.

Hannah smiled at a memory that replayed in her mind. "I remember Liz saying that whenever she had to tell her mother some bad news she'd go to you first. Of course I didn't understand why, then."

"So tell me." Mary too smiled at her own memories.

"Paul is dead. He committed suicide in prison."

May looked aghast. "Oh, Hannah, I'm so sorry."

"That's not all. I've been told, warned, that he didn't kill himself. He was murdered to silence him. It might not be true but it would mean..."

"It means there are still people out there who are linked to Liz's murder." Mary stood up, walked to the window and stared out into the street. Hannah was torn between going over to her and not intruding. She chose the latter. Eventually the older woman returned to where she'd been sitting.

"Will this never end? Hannah promise me you will be careful. He was Elizabeth's father... You may still be a target."

"I know." That knowledge left her feeling more alone and vulnerable than she would have thought possible a few days ago.

CHAPTER TWENTY-FOUR

The Reverend Martyn Jones was already in the side street café they had arranged to meet in when he had got back to her on Friday. Easy to spot, as he was the only person wearing a clerical collar, she walked over to him, noticing he had picked a table in the far corner which couldn't be seen from the outside. He had taken the seat with its back to the wall.

He stood up and shook her hand. "Nice to meet you at last, Hannah."

At last? What had Paul been saying?

"Patrick Ryan was a good friend of mine." That sentence said so much and yet so little. Where had he been when Patrick needed a friend?

"I'm sorry for your loss." Even to Hannah's ears that comment seemed trite but what do you say?

Hannah sat down and they ordered coffee from the waitress who had sidled up looking bored and miserable.

"Hope she doesn't curdle the milk." The priest laughed at the expression on Hannah's face. "Sorry, sometimes I don't realise I've spoken my thoughts out loud."

"That could be awkward in your job."

"It is – but there are times when it works to my advantage." Martyn had an engaging smile that made him immediately look younger. She assumed he was in his forties. His mousey hair, cut fairly short, showed some grey at the temples.

The coffee arrived.

"I hope I didn't upset you with my letter," he said

without preamble. "As you no doubt can imagine I counsel all sorts of inmates. Not all are criminals. If they are on remand they may be innocent, as are some who have been tried and found guilty. Many use the chapel just as a place to sit and reflect. I like to give them that space. The noise in the communal areas and," he paused as though choosing his words carefully, "a shared prison cell isn't conducive to introspection."

Hannah couldn't even begin to imagine how Paul had coped with incarceration. He had always prized his privacy and never liked to be tied down. He took care with his appearance and dressed immaculately. Communal showers and a loo in a shared cell would have horrified him. How he must have hated it. Then she thought of his involvement with the people behind all the killings and all her sympathy vanished.

"You said in your letter that you hadn't thought Paul was suicidal?"

"He wasn't. He was not depressed but he was despondent about his situation which was only natural, and he was full of remorse for what he had done."

Hannah could feel herself going hot then cold. Her stomach was gripped in a spasm of remembered fear.

"Hannah, are you ok?" His hand covered hers on the table. "Hannah?"

"I'm sorry, I…"

"Please don't apologise. It was remiss of me. I should have thought about what I was saying. Those memories must be horrifying for you."

Hannah nodded. He gave her a moment to collect herself.

"Anyway. Paul was definitely not thought of as a suicide risk. And I never had the impression that he would consider such a terrible thing." He paused to drink some coffee, before dropping his bombshell.

"I believe he was killed to prevent him testifying."

The cup Hannah had been holding clattered on to the saucer causing several people to turn and look at them. "But – I don't understand." So Mike was right.

"It was made to look like he'd taken his own life. Relatively easily done, I'm afraid, even inside a prison."

He had signalled to the waitress and two more coffees appeared along with a glass of water for Hannah.

"As I mentioned I cannot betray what was told to me in confidence. But Paul did give me your contact details. I got the strong impression he was frightened. At first I thought that was a natural reaction to being in prison. Then I realised it was more than that. He was convinced something would happen to him."

"But why didn't the prison officers protect him?" Will all this never end? she thought. Evidently MI5 had not caught all the perpetrators as they had claimed. Or as both DI Claudia Turner and Tom had assured her.

"I've already said more than I should have. I wanted you to know, to be on your guard." He watched her face. She had a little more colour now.

"You've been through so much already. I hope you have a good support network. If you ever want to talk – about anything – I'd be happy to meet up."

"Will this come out at the inquest?"

He stared at his hands. "I shouldn't think so." They were both quiet for a moment.

"Well you're not the first to tell me this." The chaplain, she noticed, didn't look surprised. "I couldn't really believe it the first time but now –" she fiddled with the sugar spoon. "This is the second suspicious prison death I've heard about within a few days."

"Oh – was the other one someone you knew?"

"Yes, the someone who had held a gun to my baby daughter's head." She forced the memory away. "I was told that it was probably not natural causes as reported. Two people who threatened my daughter's life are dead. Prisons don't seem to be very safe or healthy places."

"They're not. At least not in my experience. They are noisy and oppressive with an undercurrent of violence waiting to erupt. And that's on a good day." He smiled. "I'm so sorry for your loss, Hannah." He looked at his watch. "I have to go now. But contact me any time."

They both stood up and Martyn left some cash on the table. "How are you getting back?"

Hannah swallowed hard. "I have an appointment with Paul's solicitor in town so I'll get the tube."

As they shook hands, Martyn said, "Peace be with you and may the Lord keep you and your daughter safe." It didn't sound as reassuring as it should have, Hannah thought, walking off in different direction to the chaplain, and wondering what new revelations would be in store for her. What papers had Paul left with his solicitor?

What a complete idiot Paul had been.

The solicitor's office was just off Chancery Lane. Hannah had taken the Victoria line from Brixton changing at

Green Park for the Piccadilly Line to Holborn. Mid-morning there were plenty of seats available. But still someone sat next to her – too closely and she remembered the journey she'd made not that long ago from King's Cross to Waterloo dressed in old charity shop clothes so as to blend in with the homeless community in the Bull Ring. Everyone had given her a wide berth then.

She emerged at Holborn and took her bearings. What she hadn't realised was that the road she wanted was at the far end of Chancery Lane. She wished she had put on shoes more comfortable for walking in and set off at a brisk pace.

The white building housing the solicitor's offices was well-maintained with window boxes almost overflowing with early pansies. The offices were on the first floor. A receptionist greeted her and phoned through to Neville Rogers who came out to meet her. He was younger than she'd imagined from his voice. Just an inch or so taller than her, he clutched her hand and she noticed the nicotine stains on his fingers. His office was medium-sized. Light and airy. No smell of cigarettes to Hannah's relief.

"Please sit down, Ms Weybridge." He fussed about with some papers on his desk, coughed and then, as though to delay what he had to say, offered her tea or coffee.

"No thank you," Hannah replied. She waited.

Rogers coughed again. "You may or may not know that Paul Montague's assets were frozen when he was put on remand. It will take some time to sort all that out. He did, however, ask me to organise some life assurance a while ago which I did. His daughter..." Hannah bristled at the use of that word but was aware that Rogers was watching her reaction and said nothing. "Elizabeth is the sole beneficiary of that money. It will be held in trust for her until she is eighteen."

Hannah was about to say that she didn't want his money but of course it wasn't hers to reject. It was Elizabeth's. "Are there any conditions?"

"None at all." Mr Rogers' smile looked practiced as though at some time he had stood in front of a mirror working out the most appropriate expressions to mould his face into for each and every occasion which arose.

"Fine. So who are the trustees?" Hannah knew how rude she sounded but was unable to temper her irritation.

"I am and the other is a Dr James ..."

"James! James knew about this?" How typically snide of Paul.

"Well yes, of course. He had to, as an executor."

Furious at what she saw as James' betrayal, Hannah stood up to leave. "If there's nothing more, Mr Rogers?"

Neville Rogers stood facing her. "I'm sorry this has all been a terrible shock for you. For all of us. I was a friend of Paul's – we have, had, known each other for years and it never occurred to me that he would ..."

"Supposing he didn't." Discretion had given way to Hannah's fury.

"Didn't what? Kill himself?" He looked confused.

"Perhaps he was killed to stop him giving evidence and it was made to look like suicide?" Hannah regretted her outburst immediately but wanted to see this man's reaction.

"That is a possibility," Rogers said very slowly. "I did wonder... Please sit down, Ms Weybridge, there's something else."

Reluctantly Hannah sat, as did Neville Rogers. "I also have an envelope addressed to you which I was instructed to hand over to you personally."

He gave her a manila A4 envelope. On the front in Paul's handwriting was inscribed: *To Hannah Weybridge. Please open in the presence of Neville Rogers.*

Hannah stared at the envelope and then at the solicitor. She remembered the letter she'd been given from Liz sometime after she'd died. The terrible revelations that had led to... She breathed deeply before opening the envelope with trembling fingers.

Inside were two more envelopes: one addressed to her, the other to the solicitor. Plus a sheet of paper instructing her not to open hers until Neville Rogers had opened his. She handed it to him without a word and waited as the lawyer scanned the handwritten pages and then began again reading more slowly.

Hannah watched the changing expressions on his face. When he'd finished he went over to a side table and poured two glasses of brandy. He handed one to Hannah before sitting back at his desk. "You might need it. I do."

Hannah was furious at the way Paul was manipulating her. Why did he have to arrange such an elaborate charade? Hannah opened her letter. On first perusal there didn't seem to be anything unusual. Except...

She read through it again. She had always assumed that DI Turner had interrogated Paul after he was arrested. Claudia had never mentioned he had been interviewed by someone else before her. But here it was in black and white. He had been 'interviewed' by MI5. At least that is what Paul had assumed. Hannah wasn't so sure. That person had debriefed him. Told him what to say and what not to say. As Paul was being escorted from the interview, he caught a glimpse of another man going into the room via a different door. That person was the same nameless person who had threatened him with bankruptcy and worse if he hadn't agreed to their plans!

Hannah could feel the bile rising. The people ultimately responsible for Liz's death – and Patrick's – were still at liberty. And if the chaplain and Mike Smith were to be believed it would seem that they had organised for Paul to be killed in a way that looked like suicide. Or perhaps a different party had arranged that. It didn't bear thinking about.

"When did Paul give you all this, Mr Rogers?"

Neville Rogers took a swig of his brandy. Hannah did likewise. As the solicitor had predicted, she needed it.

"At our first meeting after he had been arrested. When he spoke to me on the phone he requested paper and envelopes. I was present while he was writing but was unaware of the contents. He sealed everything as you saw and told me only to open it if anything happened to him. I thought he was being melodramatic but agreed." He took another gulp of brandy. "When the prison governor rang to say that Paul had committed suicide, I didn't know what to think. All I knew was that I had to contact you. Now…"

"Now we need to protect ourselves."

"If I can be of any assistance at all. Anything."

"Thank you. I need to make some photocopies of these papers. I'll courier them to people who can be trusted not to open them and will keep them safe. I would be grateful if you would keep a set here."

"Of course."

They photocopied six sets. Hannah sent one envelope to Rory at *The News* with a note asking him to keep the enclosed envelope, addressed to her, safe. Two other sets were sent by courier to Rev John Daniels in Essex and James at the Hammersmith. She kept two sets for herself. "I'll pass these on personally," she said by way of explanation.

Neville nodded and escorted her to the front of the building where he hailed her a cab. He looked exhausted. "Take care and let me know if there is anything else you need me to do."

She shook his hand. "I will," she said hoping she could trust him as Paul obviously had. "Thank you."

CHAPTER TWENTY-FIVE

Joe stood up and waved to her as she entered the bar. Hannah had been disappointed that they weren't going to be meeting in one of the Members' Bars in the House of Commons but assumed Joe had his reasons for the change of venue. Monday lunchtime wasn't too busy and he had secured a table with a bottle of white wine and glasses ready. As they hugged, Hannah noticed how tired he looked. His smile was still as engaging but he looked unbearably sad. Presumably the death of his party leader had been a terrible shock. At least John Smith's demise was from natural causes, she thought uncharitably. The meeting with Neville Rogers had left her feeling raw and vulnerable.

"How are you?"

"I'm fine." Joe, ever sensitive to her moods said nothing but looked askance. "Really I am. I was shocked by Paul's death, of course. But he hadn't been a part of my life for a long time." She didn't mention going to see the chaplain or his solicitor. Or the revelations in Paul's letters.

"But he is – was – Elizabeth's father."

"And what's that supposed to mean? He's never been involved in her life. She doesn't know him." Hannah glared at him.

"Sorry. I was just really shocked when I got your message."

"No, I should apologise." She thought about telling Joe what she had learned. That he didn't actually kill himself. He had been got at in jail. Meaning there were still people with enough influence to organise that. But Joe looked as though he'd heard enough bad news for the time being.

"How about you? Being an MP looks as though it's already taken its toll."

"Thanks." He poured her some wine and raised his glass to her. "Don't get me wrong. I love being in the thick of things – if you can call being a lowly constituency MP that." He drank some wine. "John's death has left us all in a state of shock. Obviously there'll be some jostling for positions now. Margaret Becket is brilliant, of course, but she won't stand for leadership." He stared into his glass before continuing, "However I didn't invite you hear to talk about party machinations. I have a special reason for wanting to see you."

"Oh yes, the obvious delights of my company not a good enough reason?" Hannah nudged him playfully. They had known each other such a long time but she still hadn't met his new partner – well he was the only real partner Joe had had, as far as she knew. And she found this hard to accept. Joe had finally come out when he went before the selection panel so he must be more relaxed about being a gay MP now.

Joe placed a warm hand over hers. "This is probably not the right place to be discussing this. But I've heard some rumours –" Hannah could feel an icy tingle, the hairs on the back of her neck stood to attention. Surely this wasn't …? "Not about you," he said seeing her face pale and her eyes widen – "or anyone connected to you."

She sipped her wine. It took a minute or two for the

relief to register and permeate her body so that her pulse slowed down and her breathing returned to normal.

"Do you know anything about my constituency?" The question seemed arbitrary.

"Streatham West? Not particularly, should I?"

"No, I suppose not. It's a culturally diverse area with a high proportion of Asian residents. Most of those in our age group are second generation but there're still a good number of relatively new immigrants. They tend to cluster as far as housing is concerned. Although many are really well integrated some are less so. Especially the women, many of whom have difficulty with English. Their children who are in local schools often act as their interpreters." He paused, aware he was beginning to sound like a constituency leaflet, to pour more wine. "Shall we order some food?"

"Yes please – any recommendations?"

They both ordered fish and chips, apparently a speciality of the house.

"Why were you telling me about your Asian constituents?"

Joe looked uncomfortable. "I can't be sure about this but listening on the grapevine there's still a lot of arranged marriages with underage girls going on and it seems that some are going missing if they dissent or won't agree to a marriage."

"So how do you know this?"

"I'm a governor at a local school. There have been a couple of incidences there that have worried the head teacher." He stopped talking as their food arrived, smiled and thanked the waiter.

"Plus I received this in the post." He passed an envelope to Hannah. "Don't read it now. Eat your food before it gets cold."

They ate in silence for a while.

"It's a bizarre coincidence but I'm doing some research on this at the moment. One Asian girl was murdered in Peckham Rye Park –"

"Yes I saw your article. Strange that it was made to look like a suicide."

"Common in India apparently."

"What is?"

"Suicide by drowning, or so I was told. That case is more complicated than it looks. But I was going to say that someone has asked me for help with finding another girl who has gone missing. Linda has some concerns as well with a pupil at her school."

Joe looked thoughtful. "How about I come over to yours to discuss this? We could have a takeaway and you can tell me what you think. The House won't be sitting late this evening after …"

"Sounds good. Two meals I won't have had to cook in one day." She finished her food and pushed the plate away. "So how's life on the domestic front?"

On the way to *The News* offices in the taxi, Hannah took the letter from the envelope Joe had given her. Written on what looked like paper from a school exercise book, she read:

Dear Mr Rawlington,
I am writing to you as my MP but I don't really think

there is anything you can do. I am 14 years old and yesterday my dad showed me a photograph of the man he said I am to marry. It was a not very clear passport sized photo but I could see he is a lot older than me.

My dad told me his name is Hardgave and he lives in India.

I am to be sent out there to marry him. That's not what my dad said but I've heard other girls talking at the temple. That's what happens.

I am too young to get married. I want to complete my studies but my brother told me there is a lot at stake and I have to get married or I will bring shame on my parents and on this man and his family.

I have tried to talk with my mother but she just says I must do as my dad tells me. They had an arranged marriage and it worked for them, she says. But they are about the same age. This man is at least twice as old as me and he is a complete stranger.

I can't have any letters sent to my home as they would be opened. I go to a local school but I couldn't have a letter sent to me there. It would be strange.

I really don't know what to do. Sorry. I read in a newspaper that people can take problems to their MP so I am bringing mine to you. Maybe I can get to your regular surgery.
Pila Patel

When she got to *The News* she went straight to her desk. She glanced at the messages left for her then read Pila's letter again. Poor kid. What a horrible situation to be in. There must be some way she could help.

Rory hadn't been at his desk but when he returned he went straight over to Hannah. "The envelopes you couriered are safe. The meeting room is free, shall we have a coffee in there out of the way?"

Hannah nodded and followed him out of the open plan area.

"So what's going on?" Rory made a face at his coffee – he was trying to cut down on his sugar intake – and sat at the conference table.

"To be honest, I'm not sure. All the info I sent from the solicitor is to do with Paul and his involvement with the perpetrators of the Somali girl trafficking ring." Said like that Hannah managed to distance the story from the personal. "I think it would be better if you went through it before we say any more. But it is confidential."

"Okay – I'll take that as a compliment that you trust me."

Hannah looked appalled. "If I can't trust you, then …"

Rory laughed. "You should see your face. Of course you can trust me."

Hannah exhaled slowly the way she had been shown by the doctor. "Also, the Asian girls story is taking off. Lots of different angles but I need to do some more research first."

"Great I'll look forward to your first article then."

"Any feedback on the Amalia story?"

"Not yet – maybe you need to write a follow-up?"

Hannah nodded and followed him out.

CHAPTER TWENTY-SIX

"So how many secondary schools are there in your constituency?" Hannah was placing mats on the dining table ready for the Chinese takeaway that was due to be delivered.

"Five." Joe poured the wine. "And one of them is a boys' only school and one a co-ed."

Hannah smiled. "Well that narrows it down. Piece of cake really."

Joe handed her a bulky folder. Inside was information on each school, their demographic, numbers, latest local authority inspectors' reports and reviews, staff lists, governor names and addresses.

"Gosh this is impressive. I can't imagine that I'll need most of this."

"No, I know, but I set it as a task for my research assistant as the importance of education was something I fought the by-election on. So you can take from it what you will."

Hannah separated the papers into five separate piles – she could ignore the fifth, the boys' school. The research had also included a map of Joe's constituency with the schools clearly marked.

"So what do you suggest?"

Hannah was silent. As time was of the essence, it would be too time–consuming to write to each school and offer her services as a speaker for any careers sessions they might have.

"Could you visit each school – you know on a sort

of fact-finding, getting to know my constituency type of thing? Maybe all five schools in one day? Or over a two-day period?"

"Five schools, but…"

"It would look odd if you missed out the boys' school." Hannah drank some wine. "I could come with you, as an aide or something." One of the things Hannah had been grateful for was that *The News* never used a photo of her with her by-line. Most people would have no idea what she looked like. Even when she had been a target – twice – her image had been kept out of the news stories and she'd done no on camera interviews.

"You could," Joe replied just as the doorbell rang. Hannah checked the entrance camera. The Chinese food had arrived.

"How d'you get on with all this security business?" Joe asked as they opened the containers and sat down to eat.

"It was a bit weird at first but it does make me feel so much more secure. God knows what the neighbours think about it all. The woman at number nine has been wetting herself to get in here."

Joe laughed, almost choking on some sweet and sour chicken.

"At least that's something I don't have to worry about."

"What d'you mean?"

"I don't have to concern myself about home security – yet."

Hannah raised an eyebrow. "Yet?"

"We live in hope for the next general election."

"And in government you'd –"

"Serve in any capacity asked of me. Assuming I get re-elected, that is."

Hannah smiled. "Oh you will." She had helped out once or twice on Joe's campaign during the by-election and he was definitely the people's choice. Still a lot could happen before the next election. Much would depend on the direction of the new leadership.

"So how do you feel about me accompanying you on a school inspection?"

"What do you think that would achieve?" Joe didn't look convinced.

"We might smoke out the writer of your letter. There's no guarantee the name she gave is the correct one and Patel is a common surname. But we could ask about attendances and check if there is an overall discrepancy with Asian girls of a certain age."

"Couldn't you do all this with your journalist's hat on? Without me?"

"No, it would take too long. And there's no guarantee the schools would agree to meeting me and if they did, they might be wary. Besides it would give you an opportunity to meet the staff and future voters."

"Always an eye to the main chance eh?"

"Yes. Come on, you can charm them and I can ask discreet questions."

Joe smiled and Hannah knew she'd won.

"So," he asked, "how's the transatlantic romance?"

Hannah pulled a face. "Tom turned up unexpectedly last weekend and we stayed in Brighton for a couple of nights."

"So all's well then?"

"I wouldn't say that."

"Because?"

Hannah took a deep breath. "I'm not sure I can trust him."

She expected Joe to contradict her but he made no comment as he poured more wine, then said, "Life's never simple with you, is it?"

Hearing a rebuke where possibly none was intended, Hannah answered more sharply than normal. "You're the one to talk."

Joe stared at her.

"I'm sorry that was uncalled for. Shall we take our drinks into the sitting room?"

Once ensconced on the sofas, Hannah sipped her wine before saying, "Joe, there's something I have to tell you." She had been debating all evening whether she should tell Joe what she'd learned or not. And if so how much. She'd been knocked sideways when Linda phoned her earlier and told her that Mike Smith hadn't been at school and wouldn't be returning in the foreseeable future.

"Are you still there, Hannah?" Linda had asked.

"Yes. Sorry." Hannah ended the conversation swiftly. After what she'd learned today she shouldn't have been surprised that Mike had disappeared. She just hadn't been prepared for it and hoped he was safe.

"Go on." Joe's voice brought her back to the present.

"It looks as though Paul's death wasn't suicide. He was silenced. Someone didn't want him to testify."

"How do you know this?" Joe spoke so softly she had

to lean forward to hear him. It occurred to her that Joe wasn't surprised by the news.

"I was warned by someone who has subsequently – conveniently – disappeared." She decided against mentioning the prison chaplain. "Plus, Paul left some papers with his solicitor that outlined his fears." Again she was sparing with the details. "Apparently no one at the prison took him seriously when he told them he was being threatened. The official line remains that he killed himself."

"Does it?" Joe's voice was harsh. "I'll see what I can find out from the shadow undersecretary. He might even be able to raise a question in the House."

"Thank you."

Joe hugged her. "Are you sure about investigating this? Wouldn't it be easier to let someone else run with the story?"

"Of course it would. But it's personal and I will not be intimidated or made to feel a victim. I need to fight back. I won't let them win."

"Good for you." Joe raised his glass to her then changed the subject back to school visits and dates.

By the time he left Hannah was feeling a lot calmer, while Joe was wondering what the hell was going on and if he could ever be so brave.

CHAPTER TWENTY-SEVEN

"Hello, is that Alesha's mother?"

"Yes, it is. Who is this calling please?"

"It's Hannah Weybridge. I wondered if Alesha is free to babysit for me tomorrow evening?"

"Ah yes, Mrs Weybridge, my husband mentioned meeting you. Just one moment, please."

Hannah could hear the woman calling out to her daughter. There was a mumbled conversation then Alesha's voice.

"Hello, yes I am free. What time do you need me?"

"Could you be here for 7.30? I'll be back by ten and can send you home in a cab?"

"That's great. Thank you."

"See you tomorrow then." Hannah put the phone down and smiled at Janet who'd just come into the room. "How's your mother today?"

"Not great. She hates being a burden but there's so much she needs help with these days. It's good to be with Elizabeth – the other end of the spectrum." She paused then said in a rush, "To be honest, Hannah, I could do with any extra hours."

"But of course, I know that." Hannah wondered where this was leading. She hoped Janet wasn't looking for another job.

Janet looked embarrassed. "I couldn't help overhearing you booking a babysitter on the phone just now."

Relief flooded her. "No, I wasn't. I need to speak to that young lady and the only way to get her here without her parents interfering is to book her as a babysitter. I'm not going out tomorrow evening."

Janet looked relieved, Hannah thoughtful.

"However," she said, "there is something we should discuss."

"Sorry, I..."

"Don't be sorry. I should apologise." Janet looked confused. "Sit down for a moment, please."

The nanny looked as though she was about to attend her own execution.

"I'm aware of how much I rely on you to work extra hours and step in for me at a moment's notice." Janet remained silent. "So I'd like to review our contract so that your basic pay is higher and covers the odd bit of extra time. But I'll still pay when I need you to babysit... It means you'll be able to budget better and not worry about money quite so much. Is that ok with you?"

Janet's flushed face said it all. "Thank you." Elizabeth's voice announced she'd woken from her nap. Janet stood up. "Better see to Madam."

Hannah metaphorically kicked herself. She should have realised Janet would be struggling. With her own financial situation so much better now, she could afford to be more generous. Janet was a godsend and she'd be hard put to replace her. She trusted her implicitly with Elizabeth and she had gone out of her way to defend her when... when Paul had saved them from the explosion.

Back in her study, Hannah thought about how she could write a follow-up on the Amalia story. There was no new evidence. What had happened to Surjit, Alesha's cousin? Hannah thought about trying to contact her mother but that would expose Alesha.

CHAPTER TWENTY-EIGHT

She was missing something. Hannah couldn't pinpoint exactly what it was about Sunita, but something just didn't ring true. Hannah had glimpsed the parents at the funeral which Sunita had asked her to attend. It was in the local Anglican church. "We're Christian," Sunita had said and Hannah knew she'd been marked down again for her assumptions.

Amalia's parents looked, as one might expect, devastated, yet they also looked haunted as if by some other demons. There was strange body language between them and Sunita. At one point she thought the aunt was going to collapse but her brother reacted swiftly, supporting her with his arm, his wife on the other side. It looked as though it took all Sunita's strength of will to remain standing. To say they were a tight-knit family was an understatement.

At the back of the church, sitting on the opposite side to her, Hannah noticed Sergeant Benton. Their eyes met and he gave her a curt nod before continuing to scan the people present. She wondered what he made of it all.

She expected he would be cursing her now that the investigation had moved from suicide to suspected murder. However there seemed to be as little sense in a murder as there had been in a suicide. There seemed to be nothing in Amalia's life to have singled her out. And yet her death seemed premeditated. The lengths to which the perpetrators had gone to make it look like suicide suggested a history to be uncovered. Hannah wasn't sure she would get anywhere with the family. They were holding something back, but why? It was as though on the one hand they wanted to find the murderer or murderers but weren't prepared to expose... expose what? There was a secret, Hannah was sure. There was always a secret.

She sighed. There seemed to be no end to funerals in her life. Hannah would wait a respectful time and then suggest to Sunita that now it was a murder investigation by the police, she could bow out.

When Hannah answered the doorbell, Alesha was standing in front of her with her father standing back by the gate. Hannah had dressed as though going out for a meal so that he hopefully wouldn't smell a rat. Before she could say anything, he announced, "I shall be back at ten o'clock to collect my daughter, Mrs Weybridge. It is school tomorrow."

"Of course, thank you." She watched him get back into his car and drive off. Alesha was already in the hall and watched as Hannah locked the door.

"You're very security conscious."

"I have reason to be." Hannah smiled. "Don't worry, you're safe here. And I'm not going out."

The girl looked confused.

"I'll pay you the babysitting money, but we need to talk and I'd like your help."

Mr Singh had rung the doorbell at ten o'clock on the dot. Hannah worried that he'd been sitting outside in his car for some time and would have expected to see her return to the house. However he seemed unsuspicious as Hannah handed over the cash to Alesha in front of him. "I hope you'll be able to sit for me again, thank you, Alesha."

"I'd love to. Goodnight."

Mr Singh nodded and his daughter linked arms with him for the short distance to the car. It was obvious she adored her father regardless of his strictures.

Hannah poured herself a glass of wine and turned on the television to catch the last of the ITV news. No major stories. She was grateful that Paul's death had not been thought important enough to be picked up by any of the nationals. Sad that Amalia's death didn't warrant much interest either. Perhaps Sunita was right about the death of an Asian girl not being treated in the same way as a white victim.

Her mind went back over the conversation she'd had with Alesha.

"You have to understand that in our culture, we must honour our family and never bring shame. We owe our parents absolute obedience and respect. I am so lucky. My parents are very lenient."

Hannah's face must have betrayed an expression of disbelief and the girl laughed.

"My father makes a lot of noise but I know he loves his daughters very much. He and Mum allow us to mix with other girls from school but that is not always the case. One girl in my class sees no television, is not allowed to go to birthday parties or even school trips. And," Alesha paused to sip her juice, "if any of her younger cousins are ill, she has to miss school so her aunties can go to work."

Alesha was reiterating what Linda had told her. Presumably the same girl. At least she hoped so. The thought of numerous girls suffering the same fate and missing school was frightening.

"And then sometimes girls get forced into arranged marriages. One of my friends last summer was taken to India supposedly to see her grandmother who was dying. But she never came back. My mum told me that she had been married there and had been left with her new husband's family."

Alesha brushed a tear from her face. "She must be so unhappy. She was only fourteen. And now my cousin is missing. I don't know what to think."

Hannah leaned over and squeezed her hand. "Perhaps it's for a different reason?"

"What do you mean?"

"I went to the fabric shop where she worked. I was told that they didn't know her but one of the assistants said she'd not turned up for work and they were told to say she'd never worked there. Could there be a reason for her to run away?"

Alesha stared at her. "I don't know. She used to tell me everything. But recently she's been secretive. My auntie, her mother, gets very cross sometimes. She is my father's sister. But she is not calm like him."

Having witnessed Mr Singh's irascibility, Hannah thought the aunt was probably a veritable force to be reckoned with.

"Tell me are there other girls you know of who have gone missing?"

Wide-eyed, Alesha nodded. "I know them from our

community… it is very difficult if a family turns down an offer of an arranged marriage."

"But there must be parents refuse a husband for their daughters? Perhaps with good reason?"

"Oh yes. That happens. No one talked to my cousin Naaz and her family when they rejected a suitor for her. Well, not for some time. But she is studying to be a lawyer and I think some of the others are frightened of her. She is very clever."

"She sounds just the type of person I need to talk to. Do you think she'd agree to meet with me?"

"I think she would be very happy to. She volunteers for a charity and would probably welcome some publicity. I will ask her to ring you."

"Thanks." Hannah paused. "And what about you, Alesha? Will you have a marriage arranged for you?"

The young girl grinned at her. "Not if I can help it. And besides I'm hoping to go to university to study to be a pharmacist. My dad is so proud he'd never let anything get in the way of my education."

At the mention of her father, they both laughed as the doorbell rang – dead on ten o'clock.

Hannah sipped her wine. Alesha was a resourceful girl, no doubt about that, and equally she came from a loving and supportive family. Intelligent and confident, Hannah hoped she'd see her dreams realised and knew that she might also have to protect her. She wasn't sure from what exactly. But it paid to be vigilant.

CHAPTER TWENTY-NINE

The taxi pulled up in front of the Edwardian building which now housed Claymore School for girls aged 11 to 18 according to the sign outside; which also advised them that the head teacher was Jacqueline Bishop BEd. Judging by the inscriptions in stone above the double doors that faced them, this was once a school for boys as well. Joe paid the cab driver and while he was waiting for a receipt, Hannah looked up at what had probably once been an imposing building but now looked as though it might be in need of some TLC if the peeling paint around the windows was anything to go by.

It had taken Joe's researcher surprisingly little time to organise this tour of schools. The head teachers, on the face of it at least, were eager to open their doors and meet their new MP.

"Okay?" Joe stood beside her and smiled. How many women, she wondered, had been led to believe they were in with a chance? Hannah returned his smile and stood aside so he could press the entrance bell.

The door clicked open and they were in a large entrance area full of boards displaying the girls' GCSE artwork. The range was impressive. Especially the self-portraits. Hannah gazed at each one and wondered if Joe's letter writer was among them.

"Mr Rawlington! How nice of you to visit us! I'm Jackie Bishop, the head teacher. Do come this way." She exclaimed rather than spoke and looked as though she'd dressed in a hurry in a dark room as her floral shirt clashed with her striped skirt which she wore unfashionably long. Hannah smiled and was about to introduce herself when she realised that as Joe's aide she didn't need to. She was almost invisible. At least for this woman. Still that suited their purposes.

They were soon seated in the head's office. Coffee and biscuits appeared on the small table.

"So, how can I help you?" She didn't give Joe a chance to reply as she carried on breathlessly, "May I say how delighted my staff and I are at your election. We are expecting great things of you, Mr Rawlington, great things, come the next general election."

Joe looked embarrassed. "Please call me Joe. And let's not get ahead of ourselves, Jackie." His smile counteracted any implied criticism. "But we are seeing great things from you and your school. Your last local authority inspection was most impressive, and you've made great improvements in areas like attendance and punctuality."

The head teacher gave him an arch look. "Our academic achievements are…"

"They speak for themselves. You're obviously a very progressive school."

"Certainly the best in this area." It wasn't so much a boast as a statement of fact.

"Yes. And yet your intake is remarkably similar to the other schools."

"It is. We've worked hard to support girls from ethnic minorities who may have different cultural attitudes – especially to girls' education and achievements – and may not always have parents who support the girls in a way we would wish. Although that can also be said of some of our indigenous population as well." Jackie sighed dramatically.

"So how have you succeeded where other schools have failed?" It was the first time Hannah had spoken. The woman looked at her quizzically but whatever thoughts were going through her mind about the 'aide' she didn't air them.

"Firstly, I have two Asian members of staff. They serve both as an example and as mentors. We run English classes for mothers/grandmothers who need help and we've set up networks to help with childcare emergencies and so forth so that they don't pull their daughters out of school to look after siblings. We have managed to get a couple of them on to the PTA and I'm hoping that one will stand as a parent-governor next term."

"Impressive." Joe placed his coffee cup on the table.

"Thank you."

A bell rang followed by the excited hum of pupils' voices as they moved from one class to the next.

"Have you ever had an Asian girl go missing?" Joe's abrupt question didn't floor her.

"No, we haven't. We take safeguarding issues very seriously here. If we hear any rumours, any rumours at all, we act swiftly. As I mentioned we have built up good networks within the school and locally including the churches and other faith groups."

There was a knock at the door and a pupil aged about 13 came in.

"Ah, Charlotte – your guide for the school tour."

"Thank you very much for your time, Jackie." Joe and she shook hands.

"You are most welcome." She shook Hannah's hand. "I've a feeling we've met somewhere before?"

"I don't think so." Hannah thought she would have remembered such a distinctive character.

"Strange. I'm not usually wrong." But she said no more as the tour party left the room.

"Well what did you make of that?" Joe sat back in the taxi and loosened his tie.

"Do you mean the amazing Jackie Bishop?"

"I do. I think a couple of our other head teachers should take a leaf from her book."

"Well, you could arrange that, couldn't you? A word in the right ear?"

"Mmm perhaps." They fell silent, each with their own thoughts.

This school had been the last on their list. The others – except the boy's school – had all registered at least one female pupil who had left abruptly or gone missing. Most of the schools had problems with Asian girls' attendance and punctuality and each head seemed to have a different take on it. One, a middle-aged woman who looked like a defeated contender in a reality show, showed little concern. She shrugged when Joe mentioned the high level of absences from mainly Asian girls.

"It's their culture, isn't it? Not much I can do about that, I'm afraid."

She looked anything but afraid. Resigned. Dismissive. She glared at them, daring comment.

Joe made a few notes and looked up. "Quite. But I'd like to think that all my constituents were encouraged to gain the best from our education system. What are your procedures when you get a pattern of absence?"

The woman snorted her derision. "We have the home-school contract. A meaningless scrap of paper if you ask me."

"So what would you do instead?"

Hannah was watching the woman's face which was a picture of self-righteous indignation. She looked at her watch. "Actually, Mr Rawlington you'll have to excuse me now. I have a senior management team meeting."

"Perhaps I could sit in on that?"

"That won't be possible, I'm afraid. Confidentiality and all that." She stood up and extended her hand. "Good to meet you. It will be interesting to see how you fare in this constituency." She opened the door and Hannah had the impression that she would have liked to physically kick them out. Hannah felt a waft of pity for her staff and pupils.

Now sitting in the cab taking them back to Westminster, Hannah thought about the male head of the one co-ed school. He had wrung his hands and looked genuinely upset when he described how two years previously a fourteen-year-old had gone missing in the summer term. He later discovered from a family member that she had been sent to Pakistan for an arranged marriage.

"I contacted the appropriate authorities – and our then MP," he said with a wry glance at Joe, "but it seemed nothing could be done. The marriage had taken place...

They did send someone from the Embassy to seek her out but nothing came of it."

He paused and stared out of his office window, which overlooked the empty playground. His expression was tortured. "I have two daughters aged eleven and thirteen. I want them to have every opportunity they can grab. And I want that for my pupils as well. All of them. That former pupil has a baby now. What hope does she have?"

Hannah and Joe left feeling increasingly despondent.

"So," Joe broke the silence. "What now?"

"Hope that the girl who wrote to you goes to Claymore school."

"That's not very likely is it?"

"I know. Perhaps you could run some sort of information campaign? With contact numbers. There must be something..."

"I hope so." The taxi was pulling up outside the Members entrance to the Palace of Westminster. "This place will be deserted, I expect. John Smith's funeral is in Edinburgh tomorrow." His sadness shadowed his face. "Are you going on to *The News'* offices?"

"Yes, I'll do some more digging. You never know what I'll turn up."

She smiled as Joe kissed her on the cheek. "Keep me posted. And we'll see you for dinner on Saturday."

"Yes, I'm looking forward to that."

CHAPTER THIRTY

DI Turner looked up and smiled at the young policewoman who'd just knocked and entered her office.

"Ma'am, DS Benton asked me to bring this straight to you."

Claudia nodded in what she hoped was an encouraging manner.

"I logged a call from King's College Hospital. Apparently there's a young pregnant woman who was brought in after a fall down some stairs. She was in a pretty bad way for a few days – it was touch and go if she'd lose the baby. But the call was from the sister on the ward. This patient, Sasha Bhat, is anxious to speak to us."

Claudia was finding it hard to keep track of the meandering. "And this concerns me because?"

"It's about the ring, Ma'am. She thinks she has information on Amalia Kumar's ring. But she doesn't want her husband to know."

"Doesn't she now?" Claudia looked thoughtful. "Okay. Lucy, isn't it?"

"Yes ma'am."

"Right, Lucy, go and change into your civvies and pay a visit to Sasha. No point in alerting anyone with uniforms. Find out what you can." She glanced at her watch. "It's a while before visiting hours so contact the ward sister and let her know you're coming."

"Yes ma'am." Lucy still stood before her looking awkward.

"What?"

"Are you sure about sending me? Not one of CID?"

"Doubting my judgement, officer?" Claudia's face looked stern.

"No, ma'am."

Claudia relented. "Look, she's probably about your age and she won't feel intimidated by you. Get what you can from her. Oh, and tell DS Benton I want to see him, please."

Claudia picked up her phone as the officer left but there was no reply to the number she'd dialled.

"Ah, Mike, come in. I've sent Lucy to see this patient, Sasha Bhat, in King's." Mike looked doubtful. "I've told her not to go in uniform – less threatening. This could be just the breakthrough we're looking for. If it is Amalia's ring ..."

Each was lost in thought for a moment until Claudia asked, "Mike, have we had the PM for Yasmin Sagar through?"

Yasmin Sagar, they had discovered, was the name of the girl found stabbed in Peckham Park. She was fifteen. Her distraught parents seemed inconsolable and they too had cast iron alibis.

"No guv. I'll chase it up." He tapped his fingers on the desk not noticing Claudia's irritation. "I can't help thinking there must be a connection that we're just not seeing."

"Agreed. But apart from being Asian and of a similar age there's no other common denominator. Not the same school. Religion. Killed in different ways... I think I might have a chat with Hannah Weybridge. See where her research is going."

Her sergeant's face told her what he thought of that idea.

Sasha was reading an article on birth plans in *Practical Parenting*. She caressed her bump and the baby kicked. She and her baby were still alive. When she'd woken up in hospital she couldn't remember what had happened until Ahmed came and said a neighbour had found her at the bottom of the stairs in a pool of blood. Amazingly, apart from the head wound she'd only broken her wrist and twisted an ankle. Ahmed had wept at her bedside, swearing he would find them a better place to live.

She looked up to see the staff nurse, the friendly one she liked, not the bossy one, walking into her four-bed ward with a girl by her side. The girl was wearing a denim jacket, jeans and Doc Martens. No chance of her catching her heel in a threadbare carpet.

"Sasha, this is Lucy. She's a police officer. I'll leave you two to talk."

Lucy sat down in the chair beside the bed. "How are you feeling, Sasha? I hear you had a nasty fall."

"I'm okay thanks. Caught my heel in the carpet on the stairs." She looked tearful. "I thought I was going to lose the baby. I was so scared."

"I bet you were." Lucy pulled out her notebook and a pen from her shoulder bag.

"I was coming to see you lot." Lucy looked at her blankly. "About the ring," Sasha said. "Pass my bag, will you."

Lucy obliged and Sasha opened a zip compartment and produced the ring everyone had been searching for.

"It's that girl Amalia's ring. It says so inside."

"So how come you have it, Sasha?" Lucy's voice was gentle, inviting confidences.

"Ahmed, my husband, gave it to me. I think he bought it from a pawn shop up the road from where we live." Lucy made a note of the address. "He'll be angry with me but my mum saw a picture of it in the newspaper and said it looked like my ring. Course I knew it was the same one because of the inscription."

She looked at the ring. Turning it over in her hand. "That poor girl," was all she said before handing it over to Lucy.

"Where will Ahmed be now, Sasha?"

"At work. He won't be in any trouble, will he?"

"I don't know. We'll just check where he bought the ring." She smiled. "He might even get a refund, you never know."

"He works at the Post Office in Peckham High Street."

"Right." Lucy closed her notebook. "Do you live in a private rental, Sasha?"

"Yeah – we've got our names down with the council but it's a long list. Why?"

"I'd make a complaint to the landlord. He's responsible for the stair carpet that caused your accident. Check with that Legal Advice Centre in Peckham. They have solicitors working there."

Sasha nodded. "I will. Thanks, Lucy."

Lucy smiled. "Take care and good luck with the baby."

Ahmed was picked up soon after Lucy had phoned through her findings to DS Benton. It was done with the minimum of fuss and his colleagues probably thought he'd been called away because of his wife who was in hospital.

Sitting opposite DI Turner and DS Benton, Ahmed Bhat looked uncomfortable. He had been told this was a voluntary interview, he was not under arrest and could leave at any time and had been cautioned. While he was being brought to the station DI Turner had run his name through the system – nothing. Not even a parking fine.

"Would you like a cup of tea or coffee, Mr Bhat?" DI Turner had never seen Benton acting so sensitively. It was a revelation.

Ahmed Bhat shook his head. "I knew it was too good to be true."

"What was, Mr Bhat?"

"The ring. I went for a drink in The Nags Head with my mates after work. I don't usually go as we're saving all the money we can for the baby. But it was Jim's birthday. Anyway, there was a guy in there who said he had a really nice ring to sell. Said it belonged to his mother who'd just died and he needed the money." Ahmed paused as though remembering the scene.

"I didn't really consider it but one of my mates took a look and when I saw it I just knew it was perfect for Sasha. I asked him how much. I gave him fifty quid for it." He put his head in his hands.

Benton handed him a glass of water. "Take your time, Mr Bhat."

When he looked up he had tears in his eyes. "It's brought us bad luck. Sasha falling, nearly losing our baby..."

"Had you seen this man before?" DI Turner's initial elation at finding the ring was fading fast.

"No, but as I said I don't go to the pub much."

"Can you describe him?"

"He was just an ordinary bloke, really. Bit older than me. My height. Spoke with a London accent..."

"Mr Bhat, there is one thing I must ask you. Your wife implied that you'd be furious with her for going to the police. Is she right?"

Ahmed looked genuinely shocked. "No. I'm cross with myself for being such an idiot. But not with Sasha. Never."

Let's hope that's true, thought Turner as Ahmed Bhat had signed his statement then left the station. They were not much further forward.

"Okay, Benton, let's go for a drink at later on at The Nags Head and see if anyone remembers this man and his ring."

"But it's Friday, guv...

"Perfect timing. We'll go early to catch the after-work crowd. I promise not to keep you out too late, Cinders."

Mike grinned. He was more of a Prince Charming with his wife these days.

CHAPTER THIRTY-ONE

Joe put the finishing touches to setting the dinner table.

"That looks splendid." Phil stood behind him, arms around his waist. "I see we're out to impress." He nuzzled Joe's neck.

"We are. Hannah's one of my oldest friends. We've been through a lot together and recently she's had a tough time. Anyway, it's a compliment she'll appreciate."

"And will she appreciate me?" Phil sounded less certain than he normally was. He knew how important Hannah was in his partner's life and if he were honest, he felt a tiny pang of jealousy.

Joe turned to face him and kissed him long and lingeringly.

"Of course not, she'll hate you on sight." It took Phil a moment to realise he was joking.

The entry-phone sounded. Joe went over and pushed the buzzer. "Come on up, Hannah."

Joe opened the door in anticipation, but it wasn't Hannah who arrived in their doorway but a courier, his face mostly hidden by his helmet, asking Joe to sign for an envelope, which he did. No sooner had he gone than the buzzer went again and this time it was Hannah and so the envelope was placed on the hall table and momentarily forgotten.

Phil stood up as Hannah came into the sitting room. "We meet at last," she said holding out her hand. "I was beginning to think you were Joe's imaginary friend."

Phil smiled. "No, I'm real. And I at least know you by repute."

Hannah looked questioningly at him.

"Your journalism." Hannah was amused at just how many people seemed to read *The News* while claiming to detest the 'Red Tops'.

"And what do you do, Phil? Joe has always been so vague about you."

"Advertising. Graphic designer. That's how we met. Joe's PR company employed me on a campaign. I'm freelance."

"And he's now got a studio here," Joe said as he brought in a tray of nibbles and drinks. The highball glasses were Art Deco. Everything Joe collected was exquisite but bought to be used. Nothing was for show only. Except the paintings. And Hannah noticed a few additions which she assumed were Phil's.

"Cheers," he said after handing round the Martini cocktails.

Phil was looking at Joe oddly. "I hope that's not the dinner I can smell."

They all inhaled, aware of an odour, which was not at all appetising.

Joe went into the hall. "Shit!"

Phil and Hannah followed and saw him picking up the package that had been delivered just before Hannah's arrival. He disappeared into the kitchen. A few more expletives followed. Joe emerged carrying a black bin bag. "I'm just going to put this in the bin downstairs."

He returned and went straight to the bathroom where

he spent some minutes scrubbing his hands before returning to the sitting room.

"Sorry about that. Where were we?"

Hannah would have loved to ask what was in the package but restrained herself. Phil went over and kissed the top of his head. "I'll serve the starter, shall I?"

Joe nodded and gulped his drink.

The rest of the evening went smoothly. Delicious food, good wine and Phil turned out to be excellent company – he and Hannah actually had a several acquaintances in common. She was grateful that Joe didn't mention Paul's death and if Phil knew he made no comment either.

On her way home in the taxi, Hannah wondered about the contents of the package. Whatever it was, was offensive. But why on earth had it been sent to Joe? Who had he offended? She hoped it had nothing to do with his being gay and openly living with his partner. Is this what one could expect by becoming a public figure?

On reflection she'd liked Phil. He and Joe seemed at ease and easy with each other. She envied them. Joe had been her friend since university. Now she felt she'd lost a part of him.

Stupid woman, she thought. You're just never satisfied.

CHAPTER THIRTY-TWO

Elizabeth slept in longer than usual, so Hannah had the luxury of being able to read in bed. When her daughter did wake, they went downstairs to find the garden bathed in sunlight. It was warm enough for them to have a leisurely breakfast outdoors. As Elizabeth tottered over to her sandpit, Hannah's mobile phone rang.

"Hi, Hannah," Claudia Turner's voice sounded remarkably friendly, "are you free this evening? I wondered if I could pop over for that drink we keep saying we'll have."

Hannah hesitated only a moment. "Yes, that would be nice."

"We could order a takeaway if you fancied it? My treat."

Hannah laughed. "Why do I get the feeling I'm being buttered up here?"

"Am I that obvious?" She didn't wait for a reply. "I do want to run a couple of things past you, totally off the record. And it would, of course, be nice to see you."

They arranged for Claudia to arrive at seven.

All day questions rose like champagne bubbles in Hannah's mind. What was Claudia after? Information no doubt but Hannah hoped it would be a mutual exchange. Why was the detective alone on a Sunday evening? Tom had never mentioned anything about her private life and Hannah had the impression she was indeed a very private person.

However, Hannah had seen a more relaxed Claudia when she'd turned up one evening with a bottle of wine to tell her that Father Patrick had been found drugged and wandering on Waterloo Bridge. Claudia had actually seemed friendly. And later Hannah had had reason to be grateful for her professionalism and determination to see justice done.

While Elizabeth had her nap, Hannah sat enveloped in the sun's heat, reading.

Claudia arrived a little after seven. "Sorry, I passed by the Indian to get a menu."

Hannah realised she had no idea where Claudia lived. "Did you walk here?"

"No I caught the bus." She brandished a bag containing two bottles of wine. "I'll get a cab home."

"So where's home?"

"Kennington. I have a flat at the top of a Victorian house." She had taken off her jacket and followed Hannah into the sitting room. "I miss having a garden to sit in but I'd never have the patience or the greenness of fingers to cultivate it."

Hannah fetched some glasses and Claudia poured the wine. "Shall we order first? I don't know how long they take to deliver."

What to eat was decided quickly and their order phoned through. Claudia paid by credit card. "So," she stared at her glass for a moment. "What I am about to tell you is off the record and totally confidential – for the time being at least. Are you okay with that?"

"Ye-es. Does that mean I get a go ahead when and if I

want to write about it?"

"Of course. In fact, we may need you to run a story for us."

Hannah pulled a face.

"Come on Hannah don't get all holier than thou on me."

The doorbell rang and Hannah checked the video image. She noticed Claudia watching her. "It's become second nature now. And our food has arrived."

They ate in the kitchen. "You still haven't told me whatever it is that's off the record." Hannah was intrigued.

"We've found the ring. Amalia's ring."

"That's brilliant! Have you told the family yet?" Hannah could imagine it would be difficult news for the Kumars.

"No, we're hanging fire at the moment. The ring was sold in a pub, The Nags Head in Peckham."

"How did you get it?"

"The young woman it was given to contacted us."

"What took her so long?"

Claudia looked pensive. "She had an accident. Fell down the stairs and nearly lost her baby."

"Oh heavens. It was an accident though?"

"Yes, she caught her heel in a worn stair carpet."

"That's a relief."

If Claudia thought that was an odd comment she didn't say so. "I was ready for that." She had finished the curry and reached for her wine and sat back in her chair.

"So was I, thank you. Shall we take our wine through to the sitting room?"

Once there Hannah asked, "So what are you going to do about the ring?"

"I went to The Nags Head yesterday with Mike Benton. Apparently the guy who sold the ring is a regular and often sells things 'off the back of a lorry'. So he's unlikely to be our killer. But we have his name. He seems to move around a lot so the address we have may be out of date. But it's only a matter of time before we find him and then maybe Amalia's killers."

"So you're keeping quiet about the ring until you've seen this guy."

"Exactly." Claudia refilled their glasses.

"Claudia, I need to ask you something. Do you know who interviewed Paul Montague before you?"

Claudia looked genuinely perplexed. "I wasn't aware that anyone else had. Why do you ask?"

"It's complicated." Hannah was unsure how much she should reveal. "I was told that Paul's death was made to look like suicide but that he had been killed."

"That's not entirely implausible. I can make a few enquiries and see where that leads." She topped up their glasses. "Also, I was wondering if you'd come up with anything about Asian girls going missing?"

Hannah decided she could play poker too. "Not much, I'm afraid. A few mentions in local papers that no one has followed up."

And with that Claudia had to be satisfied. She left soon after.

CHAPTER THIRTY-THREE

Hannah was furious. The bins hadn't been emptied – again – and the woman she had spoken to when she had rung the council was patronising at best. Hannah was careful with her waste. Anything to do with work, plus credit card and bank statements, were systematically shredded. She had been warned to do this.

She couldn't help smiling at the memory of a man she caught going through her bin a few weeks ago. She would have loved to have seen his face when he discovered the number of used nappies facing him.

"Can I help you?" she'd asked as she arrived at her house, quite late at night. There were no lights visible from the house and she knew that Janet, babysitting, would be in the dining room, using the table to cut out the pattern of a dress she was making for her mother.

The man, not in the least embarrassed, straightened up and looked at her. "Shouldn't think so, love. I threw something into your bin as I was passing and my watch fell off at the same time. I was fishing it out." He held up his watch by the strap and smiled as he replaced the lid.

Hannah had to hand it to him, he carried it off brilliantly and just wandered off up the road. But she noticed he'd surreptitiously removed a latex glove as he was talking.

Rory had warned her that someone was snooping around and asking questions about her. He assumed it was another newspaper looking for a story but Hannah wasn't so sure, especially since Judy had also warned her someone was trying to dig the dirt on her. She'd upset so many faceless people... people who had power and the means for retribution.

Thinking about the lack of waste collection she contemplated dumping a bag of nappies on the council office doorstep.

However she had bigger fish to fry and needed to go into *The News* office. As she was packing her briefcase, the telephone rang. Hannah grabbed the receiver just before the call went through to answerphone.

"Is that Ms Weybridge? Hannah Weybridge?" The voice was beautifully modulated with just a hint of an accent that suggested English wasn't her mother tongue.

"Yes, it is." Hannah waited.

"My name is Naaz Kaur, my cousin, Alesha, gave me your telephone number."

Hannah silently thanked Alesha who had wasted no time. "Thank you for calling Ms Kaur. I expect Alesha told you something of our conversation?"

"Yes she did. I would very much like to meet up with you and discuss this."

"So would I. When would be convenient for you?"

They arranged to meet when Naaz finished for the day in a coffee shop just off Chancery Lane where she worked as an articled clerk.

Although the prospect of meeting up with Naaz Kaur had improved Hannah's mood somewhat she was still feeling out of sorts. Rory was doing his best to help.

"What you need, my girl, is to get out more."

"Oh yes, Mr Agony Aunt, and what do you suggest?"

"We've had some comp tickets sent in for *Arcadia* at the Wyndham Theatre and they have your name on them. For tomorrow."

"But..."

"No buts. Have an evening out. Do something normal – something that you used to love doing."

Hannah didn't ask how he knew what she used to love doing nor did she mention the fact that she wouldn't know who to invite to go with her, especially at such short notice. It was embarrassing. And it brought back memories of all the times she and Liz went to see plays together. "Sorry I can't go tomorrow. Perhaps one of the subs could use them?"

Rory looked exasperated. "Please yourself."

Naaz Kaur stood up as Hannah entered the café. She was tall and slim; her sleek ebony hair was loose and seemed to caress her shoulders. Her dark eyes were lined with kohl and she looked as exotic as anyone could, wearing a dark grey business suit and a white shirt. She held out her hand.

"Hannah, I'm very pleased to meet you. My cousin has told me a lot about you and, of course, I know you by repute."

Her handshake was firm, her hand warm. Hannah returned her smile.

"It's very good of you to meet with me."

"Well, we have a common aim, I believe. Coffee?"

"Please." Naaz ordered two coffees and then produced a file from her briefcase.

"As you know I am training to be a solicitor." Hannah

nodded. "And I also volunteer for a charity which works with mainly young Asian women – girls – who find themselves pressured into marriage, often to a much older man they have never met before." Naaz paused to sip her coffee, which had just arrived.

"So what does your charity do exactly?"

"For extreme cases we have a refuge. This is especially for girls who've run away from home. For many we act as advocates. We also mediate for families who are put under immense pressure to marry off their daughters when they don't want to."

"Have you had contact with Alesha's other cousin? The one who's missing?"

"I can't discuss individual cases…"

Hannah stared at her for a moment. "I wonder why Alesha didn't ask you about her rather than contact me."

"She did. That's all I can say."

Hannah let that drop for the moment. "I really would appreciate your help. I've been researching how some Asian girls are kept off school to look after siblings as well as their younger cousins." Hannah watched her face. "Alesha's teacher is a friend of mine and she was worried about a particular girl."

Naaz said nothing.

"This is a long shot, but I've also been asked to look into the circumstances surrounding an Asian girl who drowned near where I live. At first everyone thought it was suicide but it looks as though it could be murder. Although there seems to be no reason or motive for either."

Naaz nodded. She wrote something on a piece of paper

and passed it to Hannah. "My telephone number." What she had actually written was: *We can't talk about that here. Perhaps I could visit you?*

Hannah handed Naaz her business card. "All my details are here."

Hannah stood up. The other woman pushed the folder towards her. "Don't forget your file."

"Thanks." Hannah tucked it into her own briefcase. "I'll be in touch. I'm getting a cab; can I give you a lift anywhere?"

"No thank you, I'm meeting someone for dinner."

"Enjoy your evening." And with that Hannah left the café and hailed a passing taxi. She wanted to get home before Elizabeth went to bed. And she also wanted to examine the file Naaz had given her.

CHAPTER THIRTY-FOUR

Naaz had included some anonymous quotes from young women who had been abused, with a note that said that Hannah was welcome to use them. She began reading a long, well written account by one of the women who'd ended up in a refuge:

"I didn't see the slap coming. The sound of it echoed in the silence between us. My cheek was stinging and felt red hot. I was sure there'd be a mark, my mother-in-law's disapproval branding me. My sin? I had asked to visit my own mother the next day. It was her birthday and everyone would expect me to be there.

"'You can go next week,' she said and nothing I could say would change her mind. 'I am your mother now and you will follow my wishes. And my wish is for you to prepare the house and food for when my daughters visit tomorrow.'

"The irony of the situation was obviously lost on my husband's mother. The violence of the slap guaranteed my silence. I lowered my head so that she'd think she'd won and would not be able to see how much I despised her.

"I vowed I would get away from this evil woman as soon as I could. Nothing had prepared me for this marriage. And I can't understand why no one had helped me. Why my parents had allowed this to happen.

"I had to hand over all my wages to my husband who gave me a small allowance. So every other day I went without lunch at work so I could save the money. If I could, I'd sneak some food out of the fridge to take with me. If she noticed she probably thought it was her sons eating the chapatis or naan that went missing.

"Fatima Khan rules that household. Her husband rarely says a word. Her two sons, Rahim and my husband Dewli rarely speak against their mother. If they do there is all hell to pay. Both usually opt for the easy life. I don't know how she manages to control the whole family in such a despotic way. She assumes her own right to rule – as a woman – but treats her two daughters-in-law as unpaid servants. On the other hand, her own two daughters are treated like royalty when they visit. It makes no sense.

"My mother-in-law stroked the cheek she had just struck so violently and I couldn't help wincing. It still hurt. 'If you work well, I will allow you to telephone your mother tomorrow.' She smiled. 'You see how generous I am.'

"'Yes Mama, thank you,' I replied. The telephone was on the side table in the hall. Locked as it always was. Only Fatima had the key – even the males of the household had to ask to make a call. I had tried to explain this to my parents, so my mother had attempted to solve the problem by ringing me. Numerous times I heard Fatima say 'Rana is not at home.'

"Well Rana wouldn't be at home for much longer."

Hannah paused in her reading of Rana's account of what had happened just before she managed to escape her husband's home and take refuge in one of the charity's safe houses. It was just one of many accounts Naaz had included. The next one sent a chill through Hannah.

"I went to the police. I told them that they were planning to kill my sister-in-law. They didn't take me seriously. But my mother-in-law listened. She knew. She locked me in a room and refused to let me out. I was there for four weeks. When she let me out to go back to work, my sister-in-law was gone. I never went back."

Naaz had given her facts and figures, which included the number of young married women who had fled the marital home where they had been abused and treated like servants – usually by a physically abusive mother-in-law. Hannah wondered about this. After all they, at one time, had been the new daughter-in-law who had presumably lived in fear and trepidation.

Obviously all families were not like this as Naaz had noted. She couldn't give percentages but it was enough that her charity ran safe houses. Hannah also saw that some of their clients went missing.

How was the charity funded? Hannah couldn't find anything on the Internet and so emailed a request to the cuttings library at *The News* to see if that brought up anything. They would presumably have to be registered somewhere. Then she saw that Naaz had indeed included a pamphlet on the charity that she'd overlooked. The trustees were listed. Surprisingly various religious groups supported their work including high profile Imams and Sikh leaders which Hannah found reassuring, as she'd heard that some leaders were deaf to the plight of these young women. And then it hit her. There listed among the trustees was Sunita Kumar. Now that was an interesting connection.

Would *The News* publish the story she felt brewing inside her, waiting to be written? This was so much more than schoolgirls missing lessons. How much had Linda known when she broached her about the subject? Not as much as she may have thought, Hannah guessed.

She stretched her legs on the sofa and pulled her dressing gown around her a little more tightly. She'd been reading for so long that the heating and gone off but she didn't want to move and risk disturbing the thoughts that were assembling in her mind. She scribbled some more in her notebook and as she paused she inhaled the fragrance of freesia.

There it was again. Freesia. Her favourite flower. It felt like a benediction. She smiled at that word. Was she being blessed?

Having read the experiences of these young women she had nothing but gratitude for her own life. How would she have fared with all these cards stacked against her? Inevitably Caroline came to mind and the Somali girls – none of whom she met, of course. It felt like a one-woman crusade. But of course it wasn't. There were always other people supporting her. Other journalists would also be waiting to take up the baton. And other newspapers had continued to expose the plight of the Somali girls trafficked to the UK.

However that did nothing to dispel her fears. Sometimes she felt so alone. Lonely, a small voice said. The house was quiet; Elizabeth sleeping soundly upstairs. But there was no one to share a simple evening at home with.

Hannah metaphorically shook herself and gathered up the papers and file she had been reading and took them to her study. Her computer was still on, so she dialled up the Internet to see if there were any emails for her.

There was one from Simon Ryan inviting her to the interment of Patrick's ashes at Southwark Cathedral. "It would mean very much to me if you are able to be there, Hannah. I appreciate it may resurrect unpleasant memories ..."

Unpleasant memories. That was an understatement. All her memories of Patrick were tainted with what had happened to Liz and then his own murder. Not to mention the horrors inflicted upon her and her family. But maybe it would help. Who knew? She sent a reply to say she'd be there and looked forward to seeing Simon again.

Hannah took her notebook with her to bed. She found that reading through notes before sleep often produced a good opening sentence in the morning – if not during the night. Her insomnia hadn't improved. Just something she lived with now. But the scent of freesia had relaxed her and she fell asleep quickly.

CHAPTER THIRTY-FIVE

Hannah decided her best way forward as far as the newspaper was concerned was to write a series of articles starting with the education aspect and the problem of Asian girls' absenteeism. She was going to use Linda's comments, which had started all this, anonymously. Her 'interviews' with Joe couldn't be used unless she contacted the people concerned. The main one – or rather the one she wanted to quote – was the head teacher at Claymore School for Girls.

Taking a deep breath she rang the school and asked to speak to Jacqueline Bishop, expecting to be told to call back; but she was put through straight away.

She had decided that honesty was the best policy so introduced herself and continued, "You may remember I accompanied Joe Rawlington on a visit to your school."

"Yes indeed. I thought I knew you from somewhere." That surprised Hannah. She hadn't given her name then and she couldn't remember ever meeting Mrs Bishop. "I saw you at the launch of The Elizabeth Rayman Trust. I happen to know Lady Rayman through our work with another charity. It's a small world. But no matter. Everything I said that day I stand by, and it can be used for public consumption. I would appreciate seeing any quotes before you go to press. But it's a subject close to my heart so any publicity ..."

"Thank you very much. Could I have your email address to send you the copy?"

Hannah was surprised to be let off so lightly. She

thought the head would have said something about gaining information under false pretences. Good for her. She'd forgive the woman her weird fashion sense and thought she was someone she'd want on her side when the chips were down. She smiled to herself at the positive reach of The Elizabeth Rayman Trust.

The article had shaped up nicely but she wondered how her colleagues – and more importantly the editor – would regard it. She had only hinted at girls going missing. That would be the next article. And she managed to get a good word in for Joe and his campaign. Jacqueline Bishop had okayed the copy.

The phone rang. Rory sounded strange. "Hannah, you know the new MP for Streatham West, Joe Rawlington, don't you?"

"Yes, we were at university together. Why?"

"There's something we need to discuss."

"Okay, I'll email my copy over and come into the office."

"Yes to emailing copy. But I'll meet you somewhere else. How about The Boating Club? Give me an hour to finish up here?"

"OK." Hannah understood the code and replaced the receiver. She picked up her cup of cooling coffee and decided against drinking it. The file that Naaz had given her was in her desk and she quickly went through it making copies of the relevant pages on her fax machine. She had half-an-hour to get to The Ship on Borough High Street and booked a minicab. They'd worked out this plan a while ago. The editor, George, well aware that for some other newspapers Hannah was the story, wanted her to have a safe place away from other journos where they could discuss stories that might be sensitive. Only she and Rory were privy to the details.

Hannah wrote a note for Janet and left it in the kitchen where she would see it and let herself out of the house just as the minicab pulled up outside. The driver wound down the window. "Hello Hannah, climb in. Where to, love?"

By using a local minicab firm regularly, Hannah hoped to provide a modicum of security. She got to know most of the drivers and she always tipped well. The actual fare was on account.

"Rum do, that Paki being found dead in Peckham Park," the driver remarked as they set off. "Saw your story in *The News*."

"She was British." Trust her luck to get a racist driver who wanted to talk.

"Yeah well…"

"And her family are originally from India not Pakistan."

"Same difference…they're all…"

Hannah didn't hear what they all were as her mobile phone rang – Rory just letting her know he'd arrived.

Fortunately the roads were relatively clear and the driver, taking the back doubles, got her to Borough High Street in record time. She was tempted not give a tip but thought better of it. You never knew when you wanted someone onside.

**

Rory was sitting nursing a pint and got up to buy a glass of wine for Hannah.

"So what's this about Joe Rawlington?"

"You're not going to like this – his partner was arrested yesterday."

"What? That can't be true." Hannah couldn't imagine what a freelance graphic designer would get arrested for.

"'Fraid so. Gross indecency, allegedly. But if you ask me it looks like a set up. An Asian guy said he was propositioned in the toilets of a bar."

"But…

"He's seventeen."

"Shit." Hannah was quiet for a moment.

"I've spoken to a duty sergeant I know at that nick. Classic scam. Philip Tyrell went into the gents and our accuser followed him in. Happened to have someone with a camera along too."

"But surely Phil didn't incriminate himself? In a public loo?"

"No, of course he didn't. It was a total set up to make it seem as though Philip Tyrell was soliciting."

"Well I think someone is trying to warn Joe off. His maiden speech was about Asian girls going missing from school, and the importance of protecting all our citizens and making sure they have equal opportunities whatever their ethnic background."

"All very laudable. Anything else you know?"

"No." Should she mention the obnoxious smelling parcel delivered to his flat the evening she went to dinner? She decided against it. "I went with him on a fact-finding tour of the schools in his constituency. The attitudes of some of the schools are pretty depressing. And coincidently a friend who teaches is also worried about the Asian girls in her classes. It's all in the article I emailed."

"Ok – haven't had a chance to look at it yet. So it doesn't look like a coincidence that it was a young Asian guy. It was a clear message." Rory looked thoughtful. "There's a blackout on this news for the moment. Joe has the backing of his party whip. While it suits them. He isn't the story – yet."

"That doesn't sound very reassuring." Hannah's heart went out to her friend. The fear of this was exactly what had kept him out of standing for office in the past.

"It's better than nothing, believe me. Now," he reached for her hand and made to kiss her cheek. "Don't worry I'm not coming on to you," he whispered into her ear. "There's a guy over there who hasn't taken his eyes off you, so play along." He sat back. "I'll get us another drink."

Hannah smiled up at Rory who planted a kiss on her forehead then made for the bar.

In the dim light, Hannah couldn't make out the features of the man watching them. He folded his newspaper, as though he was about to do a crossword, his pen poised. Another man came in, got a drink and then sat at the same table. The first man didn't acknowledge him but stood and departed leaving his newspaper on the table. Hannah noticed that the second man pulled it towards him. Then he too looked as though he was working on the cryptic clues.

She wondered if the whole scenario had been acted out for her benefit. Trying to make her feel watched. But why would anyone do that? Paranoia, she consoled herself, it's contagious. Then she noticed someone else about to leave and the man got up and followed him out...

Rory returned with their drinks.

"That man left."

"Mm, I noticed." He swallowed some beer.

"I know this sounds far-fetched, but I think that was set up to intimidate me. They got to Paul in prison. I'd be an easier target."

"Or maybe someone is trying to reassure you. You are being watched to protect you?"

"Can't say that makes me feel much better. Shall we get something to eat otherwise this wine will go straight to my head."

They ordered some sandwiches and while they were waiting Rory asked, "What do you think about Jane selling up and going to Cork?"

Hannah stared at a circle of condensation on her glass. "I'm not sure actually. It seemed rather sudden. But with everything that happened after she returned to London, I sort of lost track of her movements." And she mine, Hannah thought.

"Rumour has it that Chris was fired from his job."

Hannah didn't say anything. The house on the outskirts of Cork belonged to Chris, left to him by his grandmother. So if he'd lost his job, maybe it made sense to move there and sell up in London.

"Drugs."

"I'm sorry?"

"He was fired for taking drugs while at work. He was..."

"Wait a minute, how do you know all this?"

"Jane told me."

"Then why ask me about it?" Hannah felt hurt that Jane hadn't been able to confide in her. She hadn't seemed unduly worried the last time they'd met. Although she had disappeared soon afterwards. They'd kept in touch, after a fashion, via email. It made Hannah feel even more isolated.

Rory was studying her face. When their eyes met, she smiled at him. "Sorry. I didn't mean to be rude."

"Yes, you did. But so what?" The sandwiches arrived. "Tuck in, being hungry makes you irritable."

Hannah laughed. "Anyway back to Joe. Is there anything I can do?"

"Think you know the answer to that one, Hannah. Widen your investigations. Keep digging."

"I've got the material for the next article. It makes difficult reading." Hannah finished her wine. "D'you know, that story George sent me on the miracle premature baby who survived? It felt so good writing about happiness. Not digging for incriminating facts and worrying that people are setting you up."

"I know – women's mag stuff." He winked. "But you'd soon get bored with it."

"Maybe. Also, Mike Laurel took the photos. Is he on the level?"

"What do you mean?"

"He seems a bit sleazy to me."

"Hannah, he's a freelance photographer. He goes

where the money is and sometimes it's in the murkier side of life."

"Yes, well, I think he's creepy and he asked me out."

Rory almost choked on the last mouthful of his beer. "For heaven's sake Hannah, you can't hold that against him. You're an attractive woman. Why shouldn't he ask you out?"

Hannah collected her things together. "No reason. Would you take these copies of the info on the safe houses that –" she was about to say Naaz gave me and corrected her slip in time – "I was given?"

"Sure." He tucked them into his jacket pocket and they walked to the door. "Try not to worry about Joe. And reassure him if he contacts you. So far he isn't the news."

Hannah hugged him. "Thanks, Rory."

Rory watched her walking down the street. He looked across the road and saw the man who had been watching them in the pub...

He flagged a taxi and once inside made a call. "She's definitely being tailed." What was she on to now?

Joe sat down wearily and loosened his tie. It had been a long session in the House. And then the meeting with the chief whip the previous evening. He'd had no idea why he had been summoned and nearly collapsed when he was told about Phil's arrest. The chief whip had offered him a drink and had reassured him that he had the party's backing, but he had been rigorously questioned about his 'social life' and Phil's. There were no skeletons in his closet Joe thought bitterly, but it seemed his security clearance might be compromised.

He smiled across at Phil who looked haggard. Never should he have doubted him for a second as he had done in the whip's office. He had hoped they were in this together, for the long haul. Now he wondered if he really could have a private life as a public person.

"I'm so sorry, Phil, it's me they're after, not you. And I won't be intimidated or blackmailed."

"That's not much consolation." Phil ran his hands through his hair. After his arrest and subsequent release he'd come home and showered, scrubbing his body trying to rid himself of the stench of the cell he'd been held in. "I've never been so humiliated in my life. I..."

Joe felt snared in a mesh of sadness. "I'll understand if you don't want to stay."

Phil looked up, his face furious. "Do you think I'd let those scum dictate how I live my life? I thought you knew me better than that."

"I do. I just wanted to – oh I don't know – give you a get-out clause."

He thought of Hannah, what she had been through, and wondered not for the first time where she found her strength. "Come on," he said. "How about a nightcap before bed? You look like you could do with one and I know I do."

As Joe poured the drinks, he looked out across the London nightscape. "I am sorry, Phil. You were targeted because of me. But I can't stop wondering what the hell is really going on? What hornet's nest have I inadvertently stirred up?" He turned in time to see Phil brushing away his tears.

"Whatever it is, Joe you can't stop now or they – whoever they are – will have won."

CHAPTER THIRTY-SIX

Hannah's story on Asian girls missing out on their schooling made page four – the home news. It wasn't a dramatic piece like Amalia's story but it was a hare to set off the hounds. Or she hoped it was.

Her second article in the series hit a more dramatic note, using the facts Naaz had given her and quoting from the young women in the refuge who had escaped from abusive husbands or mothers-in-law. In the hope of finding out more, Hannah had rung Sunita and asked her about her connection to the charity which set up the women's refuges. She was given short shrift.

"I have more pressing concerns, Hannah, in case you have forgotten. The police are doing nothing to find my niece's murderers…"

"You don't know that."

"Don't I? I have telephoned numerous times but I am given the brush off. And what are you doing? Writing about girls who take time out of school –" Hannah supposed she shouldn't have been surprised that Sunita was following what she was writing but she was stung by her tone. "Wasting your time and newspaper ink."

"I'm sorry you think that. I am paid by the newspaper, Sunita, not you." Thank God, she added under her breath. "I sincerely hope Amalia's killers will be brought to justice."

"A vain hope, I fear. We are invisible."

"That is why I wrote about the girls who miss school and go missing. Plus the girls who are forced into marriages. I'm trying to raise public consciousness of their plight."

"Well, you do as you see fit." Hannah could hear the tremble in her voice as she rang off and felt helpless. Frustrated on all sides.

Unable to get hold of Joe by phone, she sent him an email trying to be as circumspect as possible – she had no idea if MPs emails were scrutinised – but hoping he would read between the lines and know that she was there for him.

It seemed such a horrible irony that he had taken so long to publicly acknowledge his sexuality only to have it thrown back at him at the first opportunity. Why would Phil have been set up to incriminate Joe? He'd obviously touched a nerve somewhere and it probably had to do with the package that had been delivered to his flat when she'd gone to dinner. Was he being targeted because of his homosexuality or because of his speech in the House on the plight of young Asian girls? Either way it was unacceptable and she hoped the party whip would protect him. Seeing the time, she went and changed her clothes to go to the cathedral. The sun was shining so she decided to get some exercise and walk to the East Dulwich station where the trains ran to London Bridge.

Making her way across the concourse at London Bridge, Hannah was surprised to hear someone calling her name. She looked round and found herself in the clumsy embrace of Sam Smith – Snapper – Tom's informer.

"Hello, Sam. What a lovely surprise."

"No surprise really, luv. I transferred here from the Cross."

"Oh why?"

"Too many bad memories. And it's nearer home."

Hannah took in his broad smile and smart appearance. If anything he looked even better than the last time she'd seen him when he'd brought the bag she'd left with him at Kings Cross to a pub in Waterloo. She'd wondered then about his transformation.

"I thought it would take dynamite to get you away from the Cross, Sam."

He laughed. "Well, I think she's dynamite."

Hannah waited for him to elucidate.

"Marti and I have moved out to Beckenham. Got a little house an' all, haven't we. So working at London Bridge makes sense."

Marti. Hannah remembered meeting her in a back-street café. She was reading *Felix Holt* and was initially antagonistic towards her, refusing to answer any questions. But she had phoned later and when Hannah next saw her she was in her 'working' mode. She had been stunned at the transformation. Marti had been funding her studies and her child's private education by working as a prostitute at King's Cross. The information she'd supplied had helped Hannah break through the wall of silence around the death of sex workers in the area.

Hannah gripped his hand. "I am so pleased for you, Sam. And Marti."

"Thanks. She's started teaching now. That's how we got the house." He looked like someone who'd won the lottery – twice.

"And what about you? You look tired luv, if you don't mind me saying."

"No. I'm fine. I'm just off to Southwark Cathedral. Father Patrick – the priest who was murdered – his ashes are being interred there. His brother Simon asked me to go. No idea what to expect really."

Sam looked as though he was about to comment on this then shook his head. "Well, you take care of yourself. Ever need anything you ask me, you hear? You know where to find me now."

Hannah nodded. He was one of her links to Tom. One of her few connections to him. And to Caroline.

Sam looked at his watch. "Better go. Don't be a stranger, you hear." And with that he limped off, disappearing into the crowd.

Hannah followed the directions to Borough High Street, crossed London Bridge Road and skirted the Cathedral grounds by the railings. The Cathedral had an ethereal quality in the sunlight. Such an impressive building sitting squarely on the south bank of the river. It was one of the oldest churches in London and had only become a cathedral at the turn of the century when the Diocese of Southwark was created.

Hannah was stunned by its gothic splendour as she walked into the building by the North entrance. There was a sense of peace and tranquillity. She stood still for a few moments absorbing the atmosphere until an usher came over and directed her to a chapel at the rear of the sanctuary. She joined the group of people and an order of service was passed to her. Patrick's photo was on the front and her vision misted. A hand touched hers and she looked up to see Lucy and Beano. It was almost too much. Her eyes itched with unshed tears and she swallowed hard.

Someone from the cathedral invited them to sit and she saw Simon Ryan in the front row of chairs, head bowed. She also recognised the archdeacon she'd met. There were a lot of men in clerical collars. Simon had had his brother's funeral in their home town so that his elderly parents were able to be there with the minimum disruption to their daily lives. This service was for his friends. Hannah wished she had known him better.

For someone who never attended church she felt she was inside them far too often. Liz's funeral. Visiting St John the Evangelist in Waterloo; in her mind's eye she saw Patrick. How hesitant he'd been. What good work he did for people who needed it most, some of whom were here now. She smiled at Lucy and Beano as they rose and followed the priest outside into the Cathedral Garden of Remembrance. A square turf of grass and some earth had been removed in readiness. A priest said a prayer and then invited Simon to empty the ashes into the spot. Another prayer which Hannah, standing at the back, hardly heard as a gust of wind carried his voice in the opposite direction.

Then it was over and the bishop was shaking hands and saying a few words to some of the mourners. He made a beeline for Beano and Lucy who almost made Hannah laugh by dropping a curtsey.

"Ms Weybridge, good of you to come." The archdeacon, standing beside her, broke into her thoughts.

His smile looked tired but he seemed sincere, kinder than the last time she'd seen him.

Hannah looked over to the turf. "I've never been to an interment of ashes before. I didn't know what to expect."

"Nothing spectacular. But it's where his last resting place should be, at home in the Cathedral's Garden of Remembrance." For a moment he looked desolate. "Although far too soon."

"Yes." Hannah smiled as Simon approached and shook the archdeacon's hand.

"Thank you for spreading the word, Andrew." He turned to Hannah and gave her a bear hug. "Thank you for coming. I've reserved some tables at The George Inn on Borough High Street, if you'd care to join us."

"Thank you."

He took her arm and the small party walked through Borough Market. It wasn't a trading day but there were a few stalls dotted around. On regular market days the place was busy gathering a reputation as an excellent source of produce with both the locals and tourists. Being next to the cathedral – a magnet for tourists – did it no harm.

"How are you?" Simon managed to make the question sound like a caress. His grief had moved on a stage to quiet sadness. But here he was a man with a public role. The show must go on.

"I'm fine." She paused. "Well, I'm getting there. I don't look over my shoulder all the time now." It was a weak attempt at a joke. It helped to reduce the trauma of what had happened. Those people were not going to win by intimidating her for the rest of her life.

"Good. There's something I want you to have. But I'll talk to you about that later."

They had reached the pub, the last remaining galleried inn in London dating back to the seventeenth century. According to the blue plaque on the front of the building, Charles Dickens went there when it was a coffee shop and it was mentioned in *Little Dorrit*. Shakespeare too enjoyed its hospitality, apparently. It was now owned by the National Trust and leased to the tenants. All low oak beams and small windows.

Simon hadn't just reserved a few tables for his guests, he'd booked the whole pub to ensure their privacy. Lots of people who hadn't been to the interment were there ahead of them.

The manager came over to have a few words with Simon and Hannah took the opportunity to survey the guests. She was surprised to see some others were from Cardboard City. But then she shouldn't have been as so much of Patrick's mission had been with them. There were, of course, members of the clergy who joined them. And she recognised a face or two from St Thomas's Hospital where Patrick had been a patient. She wondered if Lady Rayman and Mary had been invited. No doubt they would have declined. Their own loss too recent.

Hannah noticed the bar staff were taking drink orders and handing out menus. A proper meal was on offer, not sandwiches and nibbles, presumably in deference to the Cardboard City dwellers who would appreciate the gesture.

Hannah heard her name, looked over in the direction of the voice and saw Claudia Turner.

"Hello, I didn't expect to see you here."

Claudia smiled. "I like to tie up loose ends." She saw Hannah's questioning look. "I'm here in an official capacity." She raised her glass of orange juice. "Just checking, you know. And there are others – less obvious." She handed Hannah a glass of wine from a tray on the bar. "You look as though you could do with this."

"Thanks – not sure how I should take that."

Claudia scanned the room. "Well it can't have been easy."

"No, it wasn't." Hannah sipped the wine and smiled over at Simon. What a nice man, to make everyone feel so welcome regardless of rank or status.

She turned back to Claudia. "I don't suppose you've had any leads on Amalia's killers?"

"No, but we'll find them. I see you're pursuing young girls being forced into inappropriate arranged marriages now."

Hannah smiled and wondered what the DI would think of the follow-up article on the women leaving abusive relationships. "It's more complicated than you might think."

"It always is, Hannah, it always is." Claudia finished her drink. "Well I must be off. I hope this helps towards closure for you." Neither of them had mentioned Tom. Yet he was in the thoughts of both women. Claudia went over and shook Simon's hand then left.

Hannah joined Lucy and Beano.

"Just deciding what to have, luv. Anything you recommend?"

Hannah glanced at the menu. Simon had chosen four

main courses which would cater for most tastes. A steak was included – a rare treat she assumed for many of the guests. "What's your favourite? I think I'll have the steak."

"How would you like that?" asked the waitress who seemed to have appeared out of nowhere. "Medium please." Lucy and Beano followed her lead.

"So how are you both?"

"Same as ever luv, same as." Lucy sipped her Guinness. "Always better in the warmer weather."

"Do you ever see that man, Sherlock, these days?"

Hannah thought she caught an exchange of glances but maybe she was imagining it.

"Nah he buggered orf somewhere. Stuck up sod. Always thinking he was better than the rest of us."

Hannah wondered if they realised he'd taken a bullet meant for her but there was so much confusion that evening and there seemed no point in raking over old wounds. Their steaks arrived and they all tucked in. Hannah was surprised at how hungry she was. She had just finished when Simon approached their table and sat down.

"You've done yer brother proud," Beano said. "Thank you, Mr Ryan."

"And thank you for coming. I appreciate it."

"Father Patrick was one of the best." After that tribute, Beano concentrated on his drink.

"'Ow's yer mum and dad – must 'ave been really hard for them?" Hannah wondered how much Lucy knew of the Ryan parents' situation.

"Dad doesn't understand, and my mother has her

work cut out caring for him as neither will accept any outside help."

"That must be hard on you." Lucy placed her weathered hand over his.

He didn't flinch but placed his other hand over hers. "Thank you."

Lucy and Beano had finished their drinks.

"Can I get you another?" Simon asked.

"Nah yer alright. Better be getting back now." They stood up and Simon walked them to the door. They all stood there for a moment or two. Hannah studied their faces but couldn't make out what they were saying. Lip reading would be a wonderful skill to possess. Handshakes all round and then they were gone.

Simon returned to the table where Hannah was still sitting, bringing her another glass of wine and one for himself.

He sat down and chinked her glass. "To Patrick."

"To Patrick." They both sipped their wine. Hannah was looking across to the table where the archdeacon was sitting with some other clergy. Why had they all sat together like that? She recognised Martyn Jones, the prison chaplain, in their midst. She caught his eye but his body language indicated that he didn't want her to go over and speak to him and she wondered why.

Simon tapped her arm. "I hear you've had more bad news."

She looked at him blankly.

"Paul Montague?"

Paul was more apparent in her life now he was dead than he ever was when alive. It irritated her. She felt haunted by him. "Yes, it was out of the blue – how do you know?"

Simon surveyed the room. "I make it my business. I won't give up until every one of those concerned is exposed and brought to justice."

For one awful moment Hannah thought Simon had been responsible for organising Paul's death. Then she dismissed the idea as preposterous. However, it did mean that Simon knew that not every one of the perpetrators had been brought to book.

"Do you think I'm still in their sights?" She scratched her hand and tried to breathe normally.

Simon took her hand in his. "I can't say categorically that you are not a target now but I do know that you have some powerful connections." His expression was reassuring. Hannah could feel her body relax – a little.

"I'd like you to have this." He handed her a small leather case.

Hannah opened the catch. Inside amid maroon satin cushioning, lay a plain silver cross.

"It was Patrick's. You don't have to wear it, if you'd rather not. But I would like you to have it."

"It's beautiful." Her finger traced its outline. "Thank you." And without hesitation she took it out of the case and fastened it round her neck. The chain was quite long so that the cross was low on her chest. It felt oddly reassuring.

Simon smiled at her. "I realise you probably have to get away soon but I'd like to think we can still keep in touch?"

"I'd like that. You never know when I might need a barrister."

"Always at your service ma'am." They finished their drinks.

"There's something I'd like you to hold on to for me."

"Yes?" Simon's face was the picture of reassurance. Another person she'd want fighting her corner if necessary.

She took an envelope out of her bag. "I'd rather you didn't open this unless I ask you to, or …" she couldn't finish the sentence.

Simon accepted the envelope and placed it in his briefcase, which he'd brought over with him. She noticed that he locked it afterwards.

He walked her to the door and kissed her cheek. "Take care, Hannah, and thank you for being there for Patrick."

Hannah hugged him so he wouldn't see her tears. Then she was out again in the bright sunshine, making for London Bridge and the train to take her home. She was totally unaware of the figure that emerged from the shadows and followed her at a discreet distance.

CHAPTER THIRTY-SEVEN

Hannah caught the train with just a minute or two to spare and sat down in the first empty seat. She touched Patrick's cross, then took it off and put it away in its leather case. It was beautiful and, she surmised, expensive. Then the thought struck her: Did Simon mean God was her powerful connection? She rather hoped he was referring to an earthly power. God hadn't done much to save Patrick.

She was glad to be going home to Elizabeth. She needed to hold her close and inhale her unique essence. Feel her soft skin against her own. The love she felt for her child was her reality. It made her think of her own parents. She should make the effort to visit them in France. They would love to see their granddaughter. Soon, she thought. Soon.

As the train pulled out of Peckham Rye station, she got ready to alight at the next stop. Two other people stood at the doors. Neither looked at her. The three got off then someone in the carriage appeared to notice the station and jumped off quickly, trailing after Hannah as she walked down the path to the unmanned station exit.

She decided to walk the rest of the way rather than hop on a bus for three stops. As she crossed into Lordship Lane at Goose Green she was hailed by a couple of men sitting at a table outside the East Dulwich Tavern enjoying the spring sunshine.

"Good lord," she said to James, "I didn't think they let you out in daylight hours."

He stood up and hugged her. "Meet my new neighbour, Mark Weston. Mark, Hannah Weybridge – a journalist so be careful what you say."

Mark smiled and shook her hand. His dark hair was cropped close to his head and he had a tanned and weathered look. There was an air about him that Hannah couldn't define. He looked relaxed but she thought that wasn't his usual demeanour. "My round, Hannah. Will you join us?"

Hannah looked at her watch, she still had time before Janet was due to finish. "I shouldn't but I so rarely see James it would be a treat. A dry white wine, please."

When they were on their own, Hannah smiled at James. "So what have you been up to? I haven't seen you in an age."

"Working mostly. I'd have been studying now if Mark hadn't dragged me out for a drink."

"But you still found time to see Paul's solicitor…"

James stared at his hands. "Yes, and he told me you'd been to see him." His face, so familiar to the woman in front of him, looked haunted. "I'm so sorry Hannah – about Paul dying I mean."

Hannah remained silent.

"Shit, I thought I was doing the right thing by you, by Elizabeth. And, you know, I did like the guy. Well before…"

"I know, James. I shouldn't have jumped down your throat like that. We can talk about it another time." She decided it wasn't the time or place to mention the letters Paul had left in Neville Rogers' safekeeping. "Your neighbour seems nice. What does he do?"

"I'm in the army. Just returned from Bosnia, serving with the UN Protection Force there," Mark said returning with the drinks. "And now having some well-earned home leave." He smiled and raised his glass to her. "Actually the flat belongs to my cousin who's away at the moment so I'm cat-sitting."

Simon Ryan sat back in his seat in first class, opened his briefcase and removed a sheet of paper. It was a list of names of the people he'd invited to his brother's interment of ashes. Most of these had received an emailed invitation. The dwellers of cardboard city he'd had to alert by other means.

He smiled at the memory of having asked the stuck up archdeacon if he'd mind passing on his invitation.

"And how do you propose I do that, Mr Ryan?" His telephone manner was no better than his face-to-face conversations.

"You could visit them." He was prepared for the stony silence this suggestion was met with and continued, "Although I believe a few go to services at St John's so maybe you could pass on the message from there?"

"Yes, that would be preferable. Are there any in particular you'd like to invite?"

"Yes, but I'm not sure how successful that would be. There were some names in Patrick's diary but just put out a general invitation– all welcome including any of the congregation. Perhaps you would ask someone to give me an idea of numbers?"

"Mmm I'll do my best. And thank you for the very generous bequest from your brother's estate, Mr Ryan."

"I wanted to make sure my brother's ministry was honoured and, with the proviso attached, it will."

"Quite. You may not realise this, Mr Ryan, but I had a great respect for your brother. His death has affected us all. I am glad we shall be able to honour him with the interment at the cathedral."

Now Simon looked down the list and ticked those who had attended. He came to Hannah Weybridge and underlined her name. He liked her. There was something about her assurance on the one hand and naivety on the other. Today she looked sad and he didn't think it was only to do with his brother. More likely everything that had happened. Including the death of Paul Montague. Something else he would make it his business to look into. Nothing that had any link to his brother's death would be overlooked or ignored. Nothing.

The refreshment trolley came along and he requested a whiskey with lots of ice and a bottle of water. He decided against a sandwich but accepted the packet of peanuts which came with the drink. He had a brief to read but that could wait. He wanted to recall the images of the day. Go through them minutely – just in case.

He hadn't been surprised to see DI Claudia Turner. The police often put in an appearance, he knew. He hadn't noticed her at the cathedral but maybe she hadn't been there. She looked quite friendly with Hannah. Or maybe she was keeping a weathered eye on her. He liked to think that was the case. The DI was impressive; he had confidence in her.

Out of the window, he noticed the scenery had changed

from the urban mélange of backs of houses and gardens in various degrees of cultivation: some that could have competed with rubbish tips, others cluttered with toys and washing, a few that were mowed and trimmed, sporting a riot of spring colour. Now the landscape of hills and meadows had a calming effect as the sun's last rays blushed in the sky.

The scotch was having a soporific effect along with the movement of the train but he kept himself awake. By going back to those images. Something was not quite right and it was defeating him. He concentrated as he did when he needed to assess a jury in court, focusing on each face which went with the names on his list. Someone was missing. But there was the correct number of faces. A gate-crasher? The uninvited guest.

He sat bold upright. The man in the shadows. He hadn't made the connection. He hadn't sat down to eat and had nursed his drink. But he wasn't police, of that he was certain. Ex-police maybe? In his mind Simon replayed scenes at The George. When did the man leave? The man had departed just after Hannah. In fact, to all intents and purposes he followed her out.

Simon reached for his mobile phone and swore silently. No reception. He left it on the table in front of him checking every few minutes.

Mark was laughing at something James had said. Then he leaned forward and said quietly. "Don't look round immediately, Hannah, but do you know the man standing at the bus stop by the bookshop over there?"

Hannah took a sip of wine, then searched for

something in her handbag. She took out a compact, opened it and angled the mirror to view the bus stop. There was nothing even vaguely familiar about the man.

"No, why?" She returned the compact to her bag and touched her lapel, aware that she'd forgotten to take off the hidden camera she'd worn to take photos at the Cathedral service. In the end she hadn't bothered.

"He's been standing there since you arrived and he's let every bus pass by without getting on."

"Maybe his bus hasn't turned up yet," James commented.

Mark shook his head. "No each bus that stops there has done so."

Hannah was surprised that he had paid the man so much attention. "Perhaps he's waiting for someone."

"Could be." Mark didn't look convinced.

James looked concerned. "Anyway who'd like another drink?"

"Not for me thanks. Got to get home in time for the nanny to leave." Hannah stood up. "Really nice to meet you Mark. You should drag this worker bee out more often. Bye James, see you soon, I hope." She kissed him lightly on the cheek and made her way down Lordship Lane.

Mark had been staring across the road and watched the man set off in parallel to Hannah. "We're off," he said to James who looked perplexed but followed his neighbour up the street.

By now the mystery man had crossed the road and was not far behind Hannah. There were not many people on the street at that time of day but enough to give the pursuer some cover. James and Mark halted as Hannah stopped, and answered her mobile phone as she looked into a shop window.

Simon Ryan let out a huge sigh and drank some more of his whiskey. He'd at last had some reception on his phone and managed to make his call. And in the nick of time, it seemed.

"Hannah, I think someone may be tailing you." There was a silence. "Did you hear that Hannah?"

"Yes, I'm just at the mirror shop in Lordship Lane now. I can see the one you mean. I'll find out more and get back to you."

Simon chuckled to himself. Hannah was a resourceful woman. He wondered who had coached her or whether it was an innate sense of self-preservation. He wished Patrick had had as much. There was still a dull ache whenever he thought of his brother, but he was determined to get justice for him. However long it took. He was a patient man who played the long game – as someone was soon to discover.

She swung round. The non-descript man was taken by surprise as Hannah rounded on him and took his photo with the hidden camera. The man tried to step out of her way but not quickly enough.

"So why are you following me?"

"Sorry I wasn't following you…"

"Didn't look like that to us, mate." Mark had come up right behind him. "You got any ID?"

"What? Who d'you think you are?"

"An officer in Her Majesty's Services. And I'm asking you to identify yourself."

Hannah stared at Mark. And then looked at the man who was looking increasingly uncomfortable.

"Well, the police station is just up the road," James said.

"Okay, okay." The man reached into his pocket and produced a driving licence.

Mark wrote down the details. "Anything with your phone number on, Mr Smith?"

"What is this, a bloody police state?" Smith snatched back his driving licence, pushed James and legged it up the road, jumping on to a bus which was just about to leave.

Mark shrugged, copied out what he'd written in a notebook and handed a slip of paper to Hannah who looked remarkably calm. "Might be useful."

"Thanks." Hannah noticed he'd also included his mobile number.

As they walked her home, James asked, "So where were you coming back from, Hannah? I'd assumed you'd been at *The News* offices but given your tail…"

"No, I'd been to the interment of Patrick Ryan's ashes at Southwark Cathedral and then at The George in Borough High Street. Patrick's brother Simon had organised a meal there." James nodded in silence and Mark said nothing.

"In fact, it was Simon who rang me and said I might be being followed. That's why I stopped at the mirror shop."

They had reached her house and all three stood by the gate. James hugged her tightly. "Please be careful, Hannah, promise me."

"I promise and thanks for your help as well Mark."

"Any time. Hope to see you again before I go back."

Hannah thought that unlikely as she let herself into the house and the sound of laughter and giggles coming from the kitchen. The perfect antidote to an emotional and stressful day.

CHAPTER THIRTY-EIGHT

"So what part of tailing someone covertly do you not understand, Smith?"

"I didn't think she'd clocked me, sir."

"Really? That is why she stopped in the middle of a street and confronted you?" The menace in those eyes was disconcerting.

The unlucky man jingled the coins in his trouser pockets.

"I didn't say at ease."

He removed his hands and corrected his posture. "I was sure she hadn't noticed me. I think it was something to do with the two men she stopped and had a drink with."

"In what sense?"

"They were following her too."

"And where were you while they were having a drink?"

"At the bus stop across the road."

"How many buses went by?"

"I don't know. I didn't count. I was more concerned with keeping visual contact."

"So it would seem. And they could see you."

"Why would they bother about a man at the bus stop?"

"You mean the one who doesn't get on a bus. Do I have to spell it out for you?"

He was silent. Cursing himself for such a stupid, rookie mistake.

"So," the voice was ominously low, "a game of follow my leader down Lordship Lane was played out?"

"When she stopped and took out her phone, they were right behind me. Look, I know how this seems but there was definitely something odd going on."

"Three men tailing an attractive young woman on her way home? Yes, sounds odd to me."

"I ..." he didn't say one of the men had demanded ID and he'd given it.

"My patience has run out. I want a full written report on my desk within the hour. Leave nothing out. Nothing. And don't try to justify yourself with theories. Just facts. Within the hour. And never underestimate Ms Weybridge."

"Yes ... I mean no, boss."

His superior waved a hand in dismissal. Fortunately this idiot was only the decoy. A classic call of two no trumps.

CHAPTER THIRTY-NINE

Claudia Turner leafed through the photos in the file on her desk. Three young Asian women murdered. There seemed to be no common denominator other than that they were Asian.

Her mind went back to her conversation with Hannah Weybridge in The George Inn. What exactly was she investigating now? The DI had read her article on Amalia Kumar's death and the latest one on the missing Asian schoolgirls. She had been surprised that *The News* had run with the story. But Hannah seemed to be their conscience – to make up for all the trash they published she supposed.

Claudia admired Hannah's tenacity but wondered how long she could keep on like this with a young child. And Paul Montague's death must have been a blow. Claudia had been surprised at the suicide and after her evening with Hannah she was certain he hadn't killed himself. But her enquiries into who had interviewed Paul before she did had drawn a blank.

It made her think of Amalia Kumar's death. If it hadn't been for Hannah that would have been recorded as a suicide. But they were no further on in discovering the perpetrators. Except now they had the ring.

Nadia Chopra's death was also unexplained and inexplicable. As was Yasmin Sagar's. The couple who made the horrifying discovery may have stopped the perpetrators from hiding the young girl's body. Another devastated family. They had all been interviewed and all had cast iron alibis.

She was mulling over the idea of holding a press conference, then decided to speak to Hannah. Her research might shed some light on the murders.

Hannah was engrossed in *Birdsong* when her mobile rang.

"Hello, Hannah." The voice of DI Claudia sounded tired and flat. "Sorry to interrupt your evening."

"That's okay."

"You might not think so when you hear what I have to say."

"Go on." Hannah was intrigued.

"There was another body found in Peckham Park and I…"

"What d'you mean another body?" Hannah interrupted. She could vaguely recall a small news item about a body in the area which was both Sydenham and Dulwich Woods depending on which way you entered it.

Claudia made a clipped sound as though she were having trouble drawing breath. "Sorry – I forgot there's not really been any publicity. It was another young Asian girl. That makes three deaths and the families of the latter two are wary of publicity for some reason. Unlike the Kumars. I was wondering if any of your research would throw a light on this?"

Hannah was silent. All Naaz's information had been about young women seeking refuge. "It may do. I'm not sure. I do know that some young women go to refuges to get away from abusive relationships. I hadn't heard of any deaths…"

"It was a longshot but if you come up with any stories on young Asian girls going missing it might help me."

Hannah wondered whether she should ask if one of the girls was named Surjit Gupta but assumed she would have heard from Alesha if her cousin had been found dead.

"Of course. And can I ask you something?"

"Might not have the answer but fire away."

"Do you know if anyone is having me followed. And why?"

"Are you sure?" Claudia sounded genuinely surprised.

"Yes."

"Well, I've no idea. But I can tell you that no one has admitted to interviewing Paul before I did. There is also a time lag between when he was arrested and when he was processed by the custody sergeant. I hadn't noticed it before and I don't like it. You've got one of my cards, haven't you?"

"Yes."

"Make sure you have it handy – and if you're ever worried, call me. Okay?"

Hannah said she would and hung up. On a personal level she didn't know whether she was more or less reassured by Claudia's call. But the murders of the Asian girls were a steer in the right direction.

CHAPTER FORTY

Hannah sat on the park bench facing the pond. It seemed strange being there without Elizabeth but she needed to think after a night of very little sleep. She smiled to herself – as if the ducks were going to give her the answers she needed. She watched a family of moorhens glide across the surface. They looked serene but beneath the water their little legs would be paddling frantically to keep them afloat.

What had stopped Amalia's innate sense of preservation? It had to be linked to her family somehow. And the other two deaths could be linked if only she could find the reason.

Hannah looked up at the man sitting two benches away. She knew he'd followed her. He looked cross. Probably because he was overdressed for a casual walk in the park.

Sod him! She peered at the trees opposite. No vision of Blake's angels there. The park was so beautiful and peaceful but had harboured two recent murders. She closed her eyes. Sometimes she was so tired, as she was now, that when she shut her eyes dreams started even though she wasn't asleep.

She let the images pass. Slowly. Intermingled with her vision of Sunita's grief were images of Tom. Only a brief phone call to say things were coming to a head and he'd be home soon. Could she really trust him? She wanted to but… Her attention was brought back to the present when a loud screech broke the peace and a Canada goose almost landed on a pigeon on the bank of the pond. If only they could tell the story.

Amalia must have been held somewhere before she was brought here. And whatever happened in those hours between her capture and drowning had been enough to convince her to do as she was told and give herself to death.

Although the park was locked at night there were various routes in which opened on to the Rye. Presumably the captors would have driven into the car park. It would have been after the pubs closed or people from the Clock House might have wandered into the scene.

She thought about the two boys who had found her. If it hadn't been for their illegal fishing Amalia might have stayed there undetected for days, weeks even.

The perpetrators would have assumed that.

Her thoughts drifted to the other girl who had been found in the pond in Sydenham Woods. She had been there longer. What had led the police to search for her there? Proximity to her school, the last place she'd been seen? Yet another, older body had been discovered during that search.

There were no answers here. Hannah picked up her bag and made for the gate, nodding to her tail as she left.

CHAPTER FORTY-ONE

Hannah had just put Elizabeth to bed when the doorbell rang. She checked the video image for the front door. To her utter astonishment, Sunita's brother was standing there looking awkward and unhappy.

Unlocking the door, Hannah stood aside for him to enter. "Good evening, Mr Kumar."

"Ms Weybridge, I am so sorry to disturb you at home unannounced. I feared that if I rang you first I would lose my courage."

What on earth was he going on about? "Not at all." She indicated the door to the sitting room and he preceded her in. Seeing the photos of Elizabeth displayed on the wall, he smiled.

"A beautiful child."

"Thank you. Would you like a drink? Tea, coffee?"

"No nothing, thank you."

He sat on the sofa and stared at his hands. Silent. Hannah waited. She was tempted to ask questions but she too remained silent.

At last Mr Kumar seemed to come to a decision. He sighed and smiled sadly at Hannah. "My wife and my sister know that I am here, and they know some of what I am going to tell you. But there are other things, facts, of which they are ignorant. They will be devastated – that is, if they are able to feel any more so."

Hannah waited.

"My daughter, my beautiful, intelligent daughter, Ms Weybridge, was in fact my niece."

Hannah thought she must have misheard what he said. "I'm sorry Amalia was…"

"My niece." He sighed deeply. "My wife and I were – are – unable to have children."

"But you had…"

"No, we adopted Amalia."

"But why does this have any bearing…"

"We adopted my sister's baby. Sunita is her birth mother."

Hannah said nothing. The fact explained much about Sunita's behaviour but really it changed little else.

"You don't seem surprised."

"It explains your sister's grief and …"

"Amalia didn't know, of course. It was an arrangement that we all thought was for the best at the time." Mr Kumar studied his hands. Hannah noticed a tear, which splashed down on to his finger.

"My sister was engaged to be married but her fiancé was killed in a tragic accident. My wife and I happened to be in India visiting our parents when this happened. When she discovered she was pregnant my wife and I – we already knew we could not have children – invited Sunita to stay with us in Ealing. Her life would not have been worth living in India. After Amalia was born, my wife and I registered the baby as ours. Then we moved to our present home in Herne Hill."

"Well, I am very sorry for your loss. It must be a very difficult situation."

"Yes, and thanks to you we know that Amalia did not commit suicide. However I fear – I am certain – that her death is down to me and a decision I made." He saw she was about to interrupt and raised a hand.

"Five months ago, I was approached by a family to make an arranged marriage between their son and Amalia. Now, as you know, this is common in our culture although we had already decided years ago that Amalia would be free to make her own choice. My wife and I had an arranged marriage and believe me it has worked very well. We grew to love each other and have been very happy. Sunita's fiancé was a friend of our family. They had known each other since childhood. It was a happy coincidence they were betrothed to each other." He smiled as if at the memory then his face grew grave.

"However we were approached by an intermediary to make an arranged marriage with Amalia. I doubted the motives of the family. They have a certain influence and status but their son had no profession, little education and he was ten years older. He has ... a certain reputation. Anyway, I turned down the offer and the family took it as a great insult. I offered them a financial settlement but that too was regarded with suspicion..."

Hannah sensed she was not going to like this story. So far it had been sinister but...

"I believe they killed Amalia to punish me."

"But surely –"

"I also believe they discovered Amalia's true parentage somehow and used that against her. Maybe they threatened to reveal the truth. Amalia's death was retribution of the worst kind."

After Mr Kumar left, Hannah thought about what she had just learned. He seemed totally sincere in his belief of what had happened but was it feasible? Thinking about Amalia's death – made to look like suicide – how did the perpetrators effect it? Had they threatened to expose her family if she did not follow their instructions? There was little evidence that she had fought for her life. Had she been complicit? But there was evidence of Diazepam in her blood. Hannah shuddered. In seemed farfetched but... at least there seemed to be a motive for what had appeared to be a senseless murder. She wondered how much of this she should or could tell the police.

Her thoughts turned to Sunita Kumar having to give up her daughter. It must have been bittersweet watching her grow up as her brother's child. But at least she had the reassurance of seeing Amalia every day. She wondered about the dynamics between the three adults. How much did Amalia know or discover?

She tried to imagine her daughter at fourteen being sent to another country to be married off to someone she'd never met. What mother – what father – could let this happen?

From the information Naaz had given her it seemed that some families had very little choice in the matter. Pressure was brought to bear by their community or religious leaders and other family members. Hannah wondered what it would be like to live under such constrictions. Hell. But then she hadn't been brought up in such a way.

CHAPTER FORTY-TWO

The ringing doorbell broke into her thoughts. She looked at the video monitor and was amazed to see James and DI Claudia Turner on her doorstep, both looking incredibly serious. James, in particular, looked haggard.

She unlocked and opened the door. "Hi, this is unexpected..."

James hugged her. He smelled of soap and the evening air. Claudia closed the door behind them. When James released her, she saw that the other woman had a tightness about her face. Her expression looked as though it was held together by a thread which might break at any moment. Her eyes were too bright. Hannah had never seen her looking so, so... something she couldn't divine.

The three of them walked into the sitting room. James sat next to her and put his arm around her shoulder, as Claudia, sitting at right angles said, "There's been an accident, Hannah, Tom –"

Everything inside Hannah's body was draining out of it. Her arms felt leaden. Her face flushed. She could feel James gripping her tightly. His hand was actually hurting her shoulder. She winced. "What's happened to Tom?"

"We don't know. The intel is that there was an explosion in a café where Tom and a colleague were meeting a source. There were a lot of other people in the place... We're not sure how many are dead; how many are injured."

Hannah could feel herself floating away. This wasn't happening. Her face was tingly like pins and needles around her mouth. Her armpits ached. Breathe through it she told herself. Breathe… it didn't help. Her throat constricted and she swallowed but couldn't shift the tightness. Her chest felt heavy. Crushed. In fact her whole body was weighted against her.

She could hear James calling her name but his voice was growing weaker. There was a light but nothing more except – the taste of brandy made her cough.

James was still holding her tightly and Claudia was clutching a bottle of brandy and a glass. Did she bring them with her? Hannah wondered.

"Hannah," James's voice was like the sound of a train approaching from a distance, getting louder. "Hannah."

She turned to face him, eyes unfocussed. Then a loud sob wracked her body. "Why do all these terrible things keep happening to people close to me?"

No one replied.

"As soon as there's any more news, I'll let you know." Claudia hesitated. There was still a wariness between them. The police officer and the journalist. A connection not least complicated by Claudia's own relationship with Tom.

"I could stay with you, Hannah. That way you'll know anything as soon as I do. If you'd like me to?"

Hannah nodded. "That's very kind of you Claudia. If you're sure?"

"I am. Shall we turn on the nine o'clock news to see if anything is being reported?"

Hannah got up and turned on the television. It was the end of some comedy programme with canned laughter that made her want to scream.

The telephone rang. Claudia nodded as Hannah

stretched out her arm to pick up the receiver. "Hannah Weybridge."

For a few moments she said nothing. "I see. Yes, DI Turner is with me now." The rumbling deep voice of proprietor of *The News* could be heard in the room. "Thank you so much for letting me know, Lord Gyles." There was another pause. "I'd appreciate that. Yes, I'll wait to hear from you."

"He obviously has his own sources in Whitehall," Claudia commented, just as the BBC News broke the story that there had been some sort of terrorist attack on a café in New York.

"So far we know there are numerous casualties and some are feared dead. We will come back to this when we have further news."

Claudia switched off the TV. James had disappeared into the kitchen and came back with a tray of sandwiches. "This should keep you two going." He smiled at Claudia and then sat next to Hannah again. "Sorry, but I have to get back to the hospital. Keep me posted won't you." He hugged her tightly and kissed her forehead before clasping Claudia's hand. "Thank you," was all he said. Then he was gone.

"What did he mean by that?" Hannah asked.

Claudia looked embarrassed. "I had a squad car pick him up from the Hammersmith and it was waiting to take him back."

"Oh." Hannah scratched her hand absently. "That was very kind of you, Claudia."

"He was doing me a favour." She looked distractedly at the sandwiches and poured them both a glass of brandy. "Such a genuinely nice guy."

"He is. He was also brilliant with Caroline."

"Caroline?"

"The prostitute I met when I first interviewed Tom. He was so kind to her and treated her here when she turned up half-dead."

Claudia nodded. Mention of Tom's name, the reason she was here, reduced them both to silence.

"We could be in for a long night," Claudia said at last. "Mind if I tuck in? I've learned to my cost that lack of food blunts my faculties ... You should eat something too."

The last thing on Hannah's mind was food. But she helped herself to a sandwich. The bread stuck to the roof of her mouth and she took a swig of brandy to help her swallow. But Claudia was right, they could be in for a long night and needed to eat.

They were both dozing on the sofas when Claudia's radio crackled into life. Immediately she was the professional DI. She listened for a few moments then thanked the person at the other end before addressing Hannah. "He's alive. Tom's alive. We don't know the extent of his injuries, but he's been transferred to a military hospital. We'll know more when..." Tears poured down her face. "He's alive, Hannah."

Hannah sent up a silent thank you. "Let's hope his injuries aren't too severe."

"Yes, but there's hope now." She looked at her watch. Two in the morning. More than seven hours since the atrocity. That didn't bode well if it took so long to reach the injured. But she kept that thought to herself.

"Claudia, can I ask you a personal question?" It was five o'clock in the morning and the dawn chorus had been in full voice for some time.

Both women were awake. There had been an uncomfortable silence between them. A tension that seemed to be magnified in each breath.

"You can ask. No guarantee of an answer." Claudia smiled. Her face, Hannah thought, probably reflected her own grief.

"What's your relationship to Tom?"

Claudia stared at her hands. A tear slid down her cheek. "I love him." She looked over at Hannah whose breathing was so shallow she thought she'd pass out. She leaned forward and clasped her cold hands. "As a friend, Hannah, as a friend." It was clear from the look on her face that Hannah didn't believe her.

"When we were at Hendon together, Tom helped me out of a very difficult situation. If it hadn't been for him… well, let's just say I wouldn't be in the job I'm in today." She smoothed her skirt. "He's a good man, Hannah. Principled. But you know that. That's why…"

"That's why what?"

"Nothing. It'll keep."

Claudia's mobile rang. They both looked at it accusingly. Claudia's tone was business-like again when she answered. "DI Turner." She listened. "Right I'll be there for the briefing."

She stretched her legs. "Sorry something else has come up. Mind if I use your bathroom to freshen up?"

Hannah led her upstairs and offered Claudia her box of samples to choose from. Claudia looked askance. "From my beauty writing days," Hannah explained. "Still get sent some now and again." She handed her a towel. "Help yourself to anything."

Claudia looked remarkable for someone who'd been awake most of the night. She was wearing a fresh shirt, her hair was slightly damp from the shower, and her make-up had been reapplied.

She absorbed Hannah's questioning glance. "In my job, I've learned to carry spare shirts, tights and so on. Always makes me feel more in control. Silly really. I don't suppose any of my officers care a toss how I look. But it's a confidence boost." She donned her jacket and picked up her bag.

"I'll keep you posted about Tom, Hannah. I promise." She smiled encouragingly but neither yet knew the extent of Tom's injuries. However Claudia, from her days in an anti-terrorist unit, knew what damage even small bombs could do.

"Thanks."

Claudia gave her an awkward hug. "He's alive and he'll get the best of whatever treatment he needs."

Hannah nodded and saw Claudia to the door as an unmarked car drew up to collect her. Perfect timing as ever. Hannah couldn't imagine the DI ever leaving anything to chance. But you couldn't prepare yourself for everything. Look at Tom. She went upstairs to take a shower and sobbed silently as the water mingled with her tears.

CHAPTER FORTY-THREE

Someone gave a theatrical cough and all eyes turned to Hannah who had just entered the room, a little late for the editorial meeting.

For a moment, Georgina, the editor, looked horrified then she stretched a smile across her face. "Come in Hannah, we didn't expect you this morning and started without you."

Rory made room for her next to him at the conference table. "You sure you want to be here today?"

Hannah took her seat and nodded. This was exactly where she needed to be. The New York correspondent, Frank Boyd, would have up to the minute information on the bombing, if that's what it had been.

"Obviously, the US isn't online yet but overnight we've received reports and initial observations from Frank. President Clinton has issued a statement. We have a transcript of that. Apparently there could have been as many as forty-six people in the café. Not all have been identified yet..." Georgina paused and glanced at Hannah, then continued, "All this you have in your packs in front of you. We also have photographs of the scene."

Hannah splayed out the sheets in front of her. Her need to see the images was almost matched by her abject fear of doing so. She had to know. Knowledge was power. Her imagination could be far worse than reality.

It took her a moment or two to focus on the grainy black and white pictures that had been faxed from the

States. At first Hannah found it difficult to make out anything at all… There seemed to be a lot of black smoke against a darker interior where, she assumed, the lights must have been blown out.

Beside the doorway Hannah made out a jumble of limbs that might have made up three or four bodies. It seemed as though an explosion had ripped out part of the floor. Another photo was of a woman hugging another female. She couldn't tell if either or both were dead. Another photo showed someone carrying what looked like a lifeless body.

There was someone sitting on the kerb outside, head in hands. She scrutinised each image looking for Tom. No one was identifiable.

"The word is that it was a terrorist attack, but no one has claimed responsibility yet. Rumours abound of course but we should be careful not to add to them." Georgina looked over her glasses at them. "Print the facts and not too much speculation at this stage. We should also start doing some digging – if there were any Brits among the injured get their families' stories etc. Obviously excluding Tom Jordan."

Hannah noticed she'd said the injured, not the dead. Maybe that was in deference to her. But the dead would have their stories as well.

"Hannah, I know you'll want to be kept up to speed – but no need for you to be involved."

She could feel the bile rising in her throat. Terrorism definitely wasn't part of her remit. But the human-interest stories were. She swallowed hard and nodded.

"Okay is there anything else in the pipeline we need

to talk about? No? Right off you go then. Hannah, if we get any info through you'll be the first to know."

Hannah mumbled her thanks and left the room with the others.

Hannah knew the only way to get through this was to concentrate on her work. What she had to do was write another story – not the one Tom was involved in. But about the murdered Asian girls. Work would insulate her for the time being.

Hannah hadn't forgotten Pilar Patel's letter to Joe. She rang Jude the social worker she'd met at David and Linda's dinner party and left a message. Jude rang back within the hour.

"Hello, Hannah, what can I do for you?"

"This is a bit of a long shot but you did say you might be able to help so here goes…" She told Jude about the content of Pilar Patel's letter. "I just wondered if you might know of anyone on an 'at risk' register or – I don't know really. And I wouldn't want to breach any confidentiality."

"No problem. I'll put an alert out and see what that brings up." And with that she rang off.

CHAPTER FORTY-FOUR

Hannah was at *The News* offices early, hoping to catch the night editor before he left. She was in luck. He was still in his office next to the one Georgina used. She knocked on the door and pushed it open. "May I come in?"

Terry Cornhill looked up from some copy he was editing.

"Of course. What can I do for you?"

"I'm not sure you can do anything really. I just wondered if you had any more information on the terrorist attack in New York?"

"It's been suspiciously quiet, Hannah. No claims or counter-claims." He took off his glasses and leaned back in his seat. "How's that police inspector of yours?"

"To be honest, I don't really know. Apparently he's in a special trauma unit but I'm not sure what that means. I've been told that his injuries are extensive and could still be life-threatening. But that was a couple of days ago. It's very frustrating being so far away."

"Have you not thought of going out to see him?"

Hannah looked down to the floor. "I wanted to but was told he didn't want me there."

"Maybe for the best. I expect he'll be more than happy to see you when he's well enough to be brought home."

Hannah wasn't so sure. To her mind it was not when but if he was brought home – alive.

"The FBI keep their cards very close to their chest.

But I do have a couple of contacts. If I hear anything Hannah, I will let you know."

"Thank you. It's just that it occurred to me that it may not have been an act of terrorism but of revenge."

"Revenge?"

"Yes. Whatever Tom was working on he told me that my name had come up on a list. And then there was that man –" she could not bring herself to say the word hitman – "who had been sent over to ... to shoot me."

"I can see where this is leading, Hannah. Let me ask around. See what I can dig up. But you stay clear okay?" She nodded. "Don't give anyone – and I mean anyone – the idea that you are trying to make connections."

She blinked rapidly.

"Just keep yourself busy. What are you working on at the moment?"

"Asian schoolgirls. Some are going missing. And another one turned up dead in our local woods. Three apparently motiveless murders."

The deputy editor looked thoughtful but said nothing and Hannah took that as her cue to leave.

CHAPTER FORTY-FIVE

The black car with tinted windows looked strange parked in her road. Especially when two men got out as she approached. They were both smartly suited and looked sinister to her eyes. She felt for her phone in her pocket and Claudia's card.

"Ms Weybridge? Ms Hannah Weybridge?"

She was tempted to deny who she was and keep on walking but Leah Braithwaite shouted out to her from across the road.

"Excuse me a moment." She crossed the road.

"Hannah those men have been parked there for …"

"Leah, please do me a favour?" Hannah handed her Claudia's card. "Please telephone DI Turner and give her the registration number of that car. I can't talk now."

Leah folded her arms. "Of course." She went back inside her house and slammed the door. If Hannah had asked her to play a part, she couldn't have done better.

"What did she want?"

"Excuse me? Who are you?"

They both flashed their ID. MI5. Hannah scratched her hand.

"She was complaining about your car being parked here. She's the leading light of the local Neighbourhood Watch…

"Ms Weybridge, would you get into the car please. There is someone who would like to meet with you."

"And that person couldn't telephone to make an appointment?"

"Ms Weybridge –" the rear door opened wider and Hannah was guided in. The door slammed shut and they were soon speeding away towards central London.

The first person she saw when she walked into the room was Joe Rawlington. His smile as he walked over to kiss her cheek reassured her. A little.

"Come and sit down, Hannah. This is someone who would like to talk to you about the letter Paul left for you."

Hannah stared at the man. Never had she been more glad that she had back-up plans and that other people had copies of those letters. She remembered the way Paul had described the man who had threatened him as exuding menace. *I had never been more terrified in my life.* Hannah was gripped by an icy chill.

"Ms Weybridge, we have the documents that were left in Neville Rogers' safekeeping." He paused, waiting for her to take this in. She willed herself to remain calm and not reveal her fear. "I understand you believe Paul Montague did not take his own life but was murdered."

"Several people believe this to be the case." Hannah could feel any courage she once thought she had evaporating by the second.

"Well, some people need to be assured that Paul Montague died by hanging himself. No other party was involved, of that you can be certain."

"And what if I don't believe you?"

"Oh, I think you will. Or you will find life can be very hard, Ms Weybridge – for you and your daughter."

Joe had stood up. Hannah had never seen him so angry. "What in God's name are ..."

He didn't finish what he was going to say as the door opened and DI Claudia Turner and DS Benton plus two uniformed officers marched in, followed by the Home Secretary.

"Read him his rights, Benton."

"Clive Goodhill, I am arresting you for the murder of ..."

Hannah didn't hear the rest as she was led into an adjoining room where the Home Secretary nodded to an assistant who poured them all drinks.

"I'm very sorry you had to be part of this subterfuge, Ms Weybridge. I knew from a source – actually a person I believe you know, Simon Ryan – that someone in my department had been involved with masterminding the trafficking of Somali girls. But we didn't have any evidence until news of the letters left by Mr Montague flushed him out ..."

"Hannah, are you ok?" Joe sat next to her. "It's over now."

"In the UK perhaps." Hannah scratched her hand. "What about the US?"

The Home Secretary stood up. "I'm afraid I'm due back in the House. But I think you'll find the US connection is winding up as well. Adrian has prepared a paper for you. You can finish the story you started now." He smiled and shook her hand. "Well done."

Hannah wondered if it even occurred to him that she had lost her best friend and others had lost their lives for this 'story'.

"Need a lift home, Hannah?"

"No thanks I'll take a taxi to *The News*." She smiled at Claudia as the Home Secretary's assistant came in with a large envelope.

"I've included photos as well. Not his best angles." Hannah could have sworn he muttered, "the bastard" as he left the room.

"Thank you, Claudia."

"A pleasure to apprehend the evil piece of..." She didn't finish her sentence.

"I assume Leah Braithwaite phoned you?"

"She did. Well played."

They left via the members' entrance. Claudia flashed her warrant card and spoke to the officer on duty and a taxi appeared for Hannah as Claudia disappeared in her car.

CHAPTER FORTY-SIX

Hannah phoned ahead to alert Rory to the major story they would be breaking – the 'missing link' in the trafficking of Somali girls. He would pave the way with the editor. In the taxi, Hannah leafed through the documents she had been given. Clive Goodhill had been responsible for having her tailed. He had used government resources for his own ends. Still, that was a small misdemeanour compared to his machinations within the evil syndicate he had created and masterminded.

When she arrived at *The News,* Rory waved and pointed to the Deputy Editor's office, which was empty. He brought her in a coffee as she sat down and logged on to the computer.

"I'm not going to ask how you are – I can see. We'll talk when you've finished writing. Just send me any pages as and when and I'll sub them. The legal eagles will check the article as well."

The adrenaline was carrying Hannah along. "Here are the pics of Clive Goodhill that the Home Office gave me." She took a deep breath. "God I was so scared…"

"Channel it into your writing. Use it. I'll add the background references from your earlier articles. Everyone's on standby."

"Thanks."

Rory grinned at her. "You've done it again Ms Women's Mag Writer." He left the office shaking his head.

Her fingers flew across the keyboard as she allowed her fury to be vented. All her frustration and despair at the death of Liz Rayman, followed by the murders of Sam Lockward and Father Patrick, was pounded into the keys. As she thought of Patrick she remembered that the Home Secretary had mentioned Simon Ryan. She'd phone him later.

By the time she'd finished and rewritten some sections with Rory's help, she looked out through the glass panelling and noticed that the open plan section seemed rather empty. She phoned home. Janet had had no problem with staying on. "I'm so proud of you, Hannah, and Elizabeth will be one day too."

Simon Ryan was silent for a moment or two after she told him about what had happened. "Thank you Hannah. But I'm sorry you had to be exposed to so much danger yourself."

"Well it's over now. Thank God."

The last call was to Lady Rayman. "Celia – it's over," she said. "Clive Goodhill was the mastermind and he's in custody." She paused as the import of her own words sank in. It really was over. "My story's in *The News* tomorrow."

Celia didn't reply but she could hear her calling to Mary. "Thank you," they said together, and she could hear the tears in their voices.

As Hannah put down the handset, Rory popped his head round the door. "George wants you in her office."

She followed him to the editor's domain. As the door opened, she heard clapping and the popping of champagne corks.

Georgina Henderson actually hugged her, a glass was put into her hand and that's when her body started shaking and the tears chose to arrive. She still was no nearer to knowing what had happened to Tom. There had been no updates and neither Joe nor Claudia had been able to find out what was happening in New York. Terry Cornhill had tried his contacts but there was nothing. Was Tom even still alive? Hannah was convinced the explosion was to do with the US branch of the syndicate. But the FBI had sealed off all paths to Tom...

The News ran Hannah's story on the front page, running on to pages four, five and seven. Hannah's by-line was given prominence with 'extra reporting' from Rory. Janet had arrived at Hannah's with copies of the later editions of other papers which had picked up on the story.

The first phone call was from Neville Rogers, Paul's solicitor.

"Hannah, I am so sorry I didn't get to contact you in time. Men claiming they were from MI5 virtually stormed my office and demanded Paul's papers. When they confiscated them, one of the party was left with me to make sure I contacted no one."

"It's okay, Neville. That man had to be flushed out and he is in custody now."

"Let's hope he's not feeling suicidal." Neville sounded morose.

Hannah could understand his black humour. "I think the powers that be will make sure he stands trial."

"Well, there can't be a cover-up after your story today. Well done."

He rang off and Hannah switched on the answerphone. The adrenaline rush from yesterday had deserted her and all she wanted was to clear her thoughts – and hear about or from Tom. Yesterday's victory had left her with an aftertaste of defeat.

However there was someone she had to see. Hannah showered and dressed with care. Janet and Elizabeth had followed their normal routine and were at the toddlers' club so Hannah locked the house and walked across the road.

Leah Braithwaite opened the door as though she had been waiting for her. "Come in, come in." She beamed at Hannah.

Hannah followed her into the kitchen. "Coffee?"

"Please." Hannah looked around her. The house was very similar to her own, but this kitchen was full of plants and herbs growing from every conceivable container. It looked chaotic but charming.

"Leah, I want to thank you for what you did yesterday... I..."

"It was nothing. I'd already noted the registration number of that car. I feel privileged to have helped in a tiny way."

She went over and hugged Hannah tightly. "You are an example to us all."

Hannah wasn't quite sure what she meant by that, but she enjoyed the coffee and homemade cake in an easy atmosphere.

"Thanks again," she said as she was leaving.

"Oh, don't mention it – I'll dine out on the story for months!" Leah was still giggling as she shut the door.

Back in her own home, Hannah turned on the

lunchtime news. It was strange to hear her name mentioned in connection with the major story of the day. She switched off the television and allowed her mind to wander, seeing images of Liz Rayman, Father Patrick Ryan, Sam Lockwood and finally Paul. Her daughter's father who she'd never know. This thought led to her conversation in Brighton with Tom. What on earth was happening with him? She felt a deep sadness well up. So many losses. She allowed herself the luxury of a wallow in self-pity while no one was around to witness it.

CHAPTER FORTY-SEVEN

"I have some other information for you. At the moment it is confidential and if anyone asks me I would have to deny all knowledge. But this is a story you must make public."

Hannah nodded. "Go on."

Naaz took a deep breath. They were in Hannah's sitting room. Naaz had rung earlier to arrange a meeting. Hannah was intrigued that she'd say nothing over the phone. In fact anyone listening in would have assumed they were fairly close friends looking forward to catching up on each other's news. Naaz had congratulated her on the exposure of Clive Goodhill.

Now she leaned forward, her hands cupping her knees. Her wine was untouched. "At first I thought it was just hearsay and coincidence. But now via sources I can't divulge, I am convinced that a group has set themselves up to 'sort out' problem families. More especially problem girls. I think they are murdering girls who refuse arranged marriages, and not just in London."

Hannah could feel the goose-bumps erupting on her arms. "But why? What's in it for them?"

"Money and influence." Naaz's eyes were shadowed with tiredness.

Hannah's expression must have betrayed her.

"Believe me, Hannah, this group is making serious money." She leaned back into the sofa and sipped her drink. "Do you remember a couple of years ago a

Pakistani girl was discovered dead in some woods near Chigwell?"

"No, I don't remember."

Naaz gave her a look that said "no you wouldn't would you, because she wasn't white?" But she clearly thought better of saying that out loud. She took another sip of her drink and continued, "The family had reported her missing. Her distraught parents appeared on TV begging her to come home. Pleading with the captors to let her go. It was all subterfuge.

"When her body was eventually found the family was questioned again. Again, they denied all knowledge of her disappearance." Naaz was silent for a moment. "For a while the family seemed to be in the clear. Then the younger sister broke down at school and confided to her teacher that she had overheard her father and older brother plotting to get rid of her sister because she had brought shame on them for refusing to marry a distant cousin.

"The father and brother were arrested and eventually confessed. Even the mother was party to the crime." Naaz shook her head. "It was what is called an 'honour killing', but there is no honour in murder.

"Anyway that is when, it seems, someone somewhere thought it would be a good idea to have an execution group here. That way the 'honour killings' could continue and the family is never implicated."

Hannah must have looked unconvinced.

"In India and Pakistan it is easy to buy these services. The victims are young women who won't conform to the status quo, and in all likelihood their bodies end up where so many others do – in the Ganges. Here families have to be more circumspect. Don't think it doesn't happen, Hannah. What about the Triads in the UK Chinese communities?"

Hannah was silent. Surely this wasn't the case for Amalia?

"Previously you asked me about the girl who was found drowned in Peckham Pond."

"Yes, but her family would never…"

"But her family upset the family who wanted Amalia to marry their son…" Naaz let that suggestion settle between them.

Hannah opened her mouth as if to say something but took a gulp of wine instead.

"I still don't understand. How would they have made her walk into a lake and drown herself?"

Naaz sighed. "A misguided sense of family loyalty? Maybe they threatened her with a worse death? Who knows?"

Hannah thought about what a worse death might mean and scratched her hand. "Who are these people?"

"Men who are prepared to kill for money. I have heard of cases when a woman was sent 'home' to visit family only to disappear as soon as she arrived. She had effectively been sent to her death. The family in the UK make noises about her staying with relatives or more likely running off with a lover. Gradually she becomes a distant memory. Eventually she is forgotten."

Naaz leaned forward and gripped Hannah's hand. "You can help us by exposing these practices. Sometimes the 'hit men' come into the country, do the deed and then leave. Some are really young men who disguise themselves as women and actually come into the UK on dead women's passports."

She paused. "I think we now have some home-grown assassins as well. They have to be rooted out and brought to justice."

Hannah stared into the other woman's eyes. "Are you safe, Naaz?"

"I think so but I am very careful."

After Naaz left, Hannah opened a new word file – this was the article waiting to be written. She wouldn't mention the 'execution group' overtly yet but she would write about honour killings. Concentrating on this would alleviate her worry over Tom.

CHAPTER FORTY-EIGHT

"There's a boy here, Hannah, and he says he has some important information but won't say anything unless you are present." Claudia sounded more than a little put out. "He is adamant that you should be here."

Hannah looked at her watch. Four-thirty. Not an ideal time. "I'll have to check with Janet and get back to you."

Janet, who was at the library with Elizabeth, answered her mobile on the fourth ring. Only Hannah and her mother had this number. She was happy to stay on as long as was needed. Hannah rang Claudia. "I'll be with you in about half-an-hour."

"Thanks. I owe you one."

Hannah made her way to the incident HQ. Claudia had set up to deal with the Peckham and Dulwich murders, and was escorted by an officer through a labyrinth of corridors. He knocked on a door and stepped aside to allow Hannah to go through. Claudia and Sergeant Benton were sitting at a table opposite a young Asian boy who looked about sixteen, but could have been older or younger.

Hannah did not recognise him. Nor he her. "Hello, I'm Hannah Weybridge. You asked for me to be present here, I understand."

The boy did not smile but stood up and shook her hand. "I am very pleased to meet you Ms Weybridge, my name is Ravi Grover."

"Right, now we've got the social niceties out of the

way can we get down to business?" Benton had not appreciated waiting for Hannah to arrive.

Hannah sat down next to Ravi. She looked across at Claudia. "Could we have a few minutes alone, please?"

Claudia shook her head warningly at Benton. "Of course. Would you like some coffee or tea?"

Benton looked as though he might explode.

"Coffee for me, thank you. Ravi?" Hannah asked.

"Tea please."

When Claudia and Benton left the room, Hannah asked, "So what's this about, Ravi and where did you get my name from?"

Ravi looked at her, his big brown eyes made even darker by the dilated pupils. He looked terrified. "I read your article." This was said as though it explained everything. And Hannah didn't know which article he was referring to.

She waited for him to continue.

"And I know Alesha. She said you were the person to help me. But she said I also had to tell the police as well."

"Okay."

"Alesha said I should tell the police in front of you so they would have to listen."

That young woman would go far. "How old are you, Ravi?"

"Sixteen."

"And do your parents know you're here?"

He shook his head. "They'd kill me if they knew." He looked horrified. "I don't mean that literally but they would be cross."

Hannah smiled just as DS Benton returned with their drinks. "I think we're ready now aren't we, Ravi?"

Ravi nodded and Benton went to get his DI.

"So, what did you make of that?" DI Turner leaned back in her chair. They had moved to her office after the interview with Ravi.

"I think the kid's telling the truth. I told you I thought there was something going on with the Chopra family. Their grief was genuine and their alibis were rock solid, but there was an undercurrent of something else."

"Go on." Both Claudia and Hannah were watching him intently.

"The father was beside himself when he identified the body. He was shocked by the state of her." He paused. "I know what you're thinking, Guv, but it was as though he had expected one thing and was quite unprepared for what he saw."

"But surely that's quite normal, isn't it?" Hannah was struggling to see where this was leading.

Benton ignored her. "He said something in Punjabi and wouldn't explain. I made a note of it – sort of phonetically – and asked the interpreter. She said it meant something along the lines of 'they didn't say it would be like this'."

"So," said Claudia, "you think they knew she would be murdered."

Hannah had turned white. "I have heard about this."

Both police officers stared at her.

"It all goes back to shame and loss of respect. Sometimes this is because a daughter will not agree to marry the man chosen for her. Or if married, she tries to run away from an abusive relationship. Shame and humiliation are the motivating factors for…"

"Killing the problem," Benton finished succinctly.

"Quite. They call them honour killings but there is nothing honourable in these murders."

The ringing of the telephone woke her and brought back the sadness that had engulfed her. Her dreams had been about Tom but she had no idea how he was or even – this thought plagued her – if he were still alive.

"Hello?"

"Hannah, how are you?"

"Well, I was asleep."

"I'm so sorry but I've got some terrible news." She paused but Hannah said nothing. Her first thought was that Tom was dead. "Ravi was found hanging from a tree in Peckham Park a couple of hours ago. Made to look like suicide but … I thought I should tell you before you saw it on the news. I'll come round to see you as soon as I can."

Hannah was ashamed of the relief she felt that it was not about Tom dying. But this was one death they should have been able to prevent. She wondered how well Alesha knew him. And thinking about Alesha made her wonder what had happened to Surjit Gupta, her cousin. At least she hadn't turned up dead. Yet.

CHAPTER FORTY-NINE

The number 37 bus stopped near the turning into Stradella Road. Hannah alighted and made her way past the double-fronted, semi-detached houses, set back from the tree-lined avenue. She wondered what to expect. Sunita had sounded brittle on the phone when she rang and asked Hannah to the house as she had some important information. Hannah had told Janet where she was going – not a usual occurrence but it felt better to have someone know where she was.

Her mood matched the overcast sky. Everything was such an effort now. Just getting herself out of bed in the morning seemed a major achievement. And still there was no news about Tom.

The doorbell echoed in the hall before Sunita appeared. Hannah could hardly believe the vision before her. The woman who had always been so smart and elegant looked as though...

Hannah didn't have time to register anything else as she was grabbed from behind and her arm yanked up her back, her body twisted round by the force. The pain made her yell out which brought a slap from her attacker.

"Shut it, bitch." He was dressed all in black with a balaclava masking his face.

Sunita had disappeared into her brother and sister-in-law's sitting room. The man in black pushed Hannah to follow. The scene which met her eyes was heart-wrenching. The Kumars – husband and wife – were tied to two upright chairs. They looked terrified. But the cuts and emerging bruises on their faces bore witness to what must have been their struggles.

"I am so sorry." Sunita's voice was little more than a croak. Another man, similarly clad to the one holding her, pushed Sunita into a chair with the butt of a rifle. Hannah was forced down on to a chair as well, the man's hands digging into her shoulders.

She realised there was yet another man watching them. He too was dressed in black and wore a balaclava.

"You have been slandering us, Ms Weybridge." His accent was south London and his voice sounded as though he smoked too much.

"We want you to stop writing your fairy stories about Asian girls going missing."

"And what good do you think that will do? It's in the public domain now."

The man laughed. "In the public domain," he mimicked. "Do you really think the English public gives a toss about these girls?" He nodded at the man standing behind her. The punch came out of the blue and the blow to her side winded her. "You really must stop interfering in matters which have nothing to do with you."

She screwed up her eyes but couldn't prevent the tears seeping out.

"We need to know where you got your information. Who's been peddling these lies?"

"Journalists never reveal their sources they –" Hannah was on the floor with a boot pushing down into her back. She couldn't breathe. Her vision was clouding. In the background she could hear a woman crying, pleading...

The sound of shattering wood.

"Armed police. Drop your weapons now. Put your hands on your heads." The shouted commands came from somewhere above Hannah. The pressure on her back gradually lessened but she screamed out as the boot found her hand and crushed down on her fingers.

A shot rang out. More shouts. Curses in a language she didn't know. Hannah didn't dare move.

"On the floor. Put your hands where we can see them."

Hannah could make out what looked like a woman's ankles belonging to someone standing in the doorway. The person moved aside as the men who had assaulted the Kumars and then her were roughly bundled out of the room.

"Hannah?" A pause. "Can you hear me Hannah?" Claudia Turner's voice. What was Claudia doing there?

Hannah raised her head slowly and her eyes focused on the chaos of broken furniture around her. Slowly she rolled to one side and brought her knees up to a foetal position. Her back ached. But she was alive. She pushed herself on to her knees with her uninjured hand. Her head was spinning. She thought she was going to be sick.

"Take it easy. Deep breaths." A paramedic's arm went around her shoulder; he helped her to her feet and into an armchair. He put an oxygen mask on her face.

Mr and Mrs Kumar had been untied and were being attended to. Sunita was being led from the room.

"Hannah, I am so sorry." What was Claudia doing kneeling in front of her? Why was she sorry?

Benton stepped forward. "They're ready to leave now, Guv."

**

At Kings College Hospital Hannah had been given a thorough examination and put into a side ward. She had seen a police officer at the door.

"In spite of everything you've been through, you seem to be relatively unscathed." The A&E consultant smiled at her. "We'll have to wait for some of the tests to come through, but your spinal X-rays show nothing untoward. You have two broken fingers on your left hand and you are going to be sporting some choice bruises." He sat on the edge of her bed. "How are you feeling?"

"Horrible." Hannah didn't want to cry in front of him, but it was a real effort to hold back her tears. She had been petrified at the Kumars' house. It was hard to believe that she had survived, and she still didn't know how the police had arrived in the nick of time.

"How are the Kumars?"

The consultant's expression changed slightly. "Mr and Mrs Kumar have already been discharged. Cuts and bruises but no real damage. Miss Kumar is –"

"Is waiting to say thank you from the bottom of my heart and to apologise for what we have put you through." Sunita glided into the room. She was wearing fresh clothes and looked her usual immaculate self – apart from her haunted, sorrowful expression. She sat on the chair next to the bed. Straight-backed. She stroked Hannah's hand with its strapped fingers. "Those animals – I am appalled, appalled by my countrymen. You have done so well to expose them and –"

What she was about to say was overruled by the imperious call of "Mama". In the doorway stood Janet holding Elizabeth. The world tilted one way and then another. Janet was smiling although she looked close to tears.

Sunita stood up and bent forward to kiss Hannah on her forehead. "I will leave you to be with your daughter. God bless you."

The consultant who had slipped out of the room to give Hannah and Sunita some privacy, returned. "I have prescribed some painkillers. The nurse will bring them and then you are free to go home. I'll be in touch with your GP but any problems, just phone on this number." He looked awkward. "You may want to talk through what happened with a counsellor from Victim Support or…"

"I am not a victim, doctor…"

"Never a victim – a soldier wounded in battle." Claudia had joined them. She looked shattered but also elated. "All the perpetrators are in custody. One of them started blabbing as soon as he was arrested. Even gave us some more names. So we'll be kept busy thanks to Hannah." The nurse came in with the meds. "And now I'm going to see you safely home."

In spite of her protests, Hannah was transferred to a wheelchair. Elizabeth was delighted to ride on her mother's lap with a police officer pushing and Janet and Claudia either side. Elizabeth waved in her queenly fashion and shouted not quite so regally, "Bye. Goodbye."

Once they were ensconced in the car (Hannah hadn't failed to notice the police escort but didn't comment) Hannah turned to Claudia who was sitting next to her. "I know we have so much to go through. But just one thing – how did you know?"

"Benton made something of a breakthrough with one of the families. What they revealed convinced him you were in danger. He went to your home and when he found out you had left to visit the Kumars he instigated the armed response team. A long shot which paid off."

"Well I never thought I'd be thanking DS Benton for saving my life." Hannah chuckled.

"Don't worry, it's not a complete conversion. He's going to give you hell for keeping things to yourself."

"I can live with that."

The car and escort drew up outside her house. There was an enormous bouquet of flowers in front of the door and a police officer standing to one side.

"Hope he wasn't put on flower guarding duty." Hannah's weak attempt at a joke brought a sniff from Janet who was sitting in the front. She got out first, unlocking the door and switching off the alarm before coming back for Elizabeth. Claudia helped Hannah inside. "We'll talk but not now. The officer outside will leave with us. But there's an observation unit parked across the road." She hugged Hannah then let herself out.

"There's just one thing I do need to tell you…" Claudia looked sheepish. "Ravi isn't dead."

"What!" Relief, joy, fury all competed in a whirl of emotions.

"He was found hanging in Peckham Park but he wasn't dead. The person who found him got him down in time, saved his life. But we announced that he'd died on arrival at hospital. That was a ruse, I'm afraid. To protect him and to make the perpetrators think they were in the clear. Ravi and his family were taken to a safe house as a precaution. He gave us detailed descriptions of his attackers. And he knew one of the men so we had a name."

"Who?" Hannah didn't know why she had asked it was highly unlikely she would know him.

"One of the men who attacked you. We didn't get to him soon enough I'm afraid. I'm sorry."

Hannah was dozing on the sofa when Janet came into the sitting room carrying a tray. "I know you're going to say you're not hungry, but your tablets say to be taken after or with food. I've made you fish pie – comfort food that will slip down." She waited for Hannah to move into a more upright position and placed the tray on her lap.

"Where's Elizabeth?"

"Asleep in bed."

"God what time is it? I'm so sorry Janet, you should have left ages ago. Why didn't you wake me?"

"I have now – with food. And if you don't mind, I'll join you."

Hannah watched her leave the room and return with a second tray. She sat on the other sofa. "Come on, eat up."

Hannah did as she was told. In spite of thinking she wouldn't be able to swallow a mouthful, she finished the meal and considered Janet.

"Who's with your mother?"

"My sister. I phoned her and told her she had to help."

"Good for you, but I wish it wasn't on my account."

Janet placed her tray on the coffee table and passed Hannah a glass of water and her tablets.

"Now do you need a hand with anything before I leave?"

Hannah shook her head. "Thank you so much, Janet. It was so good to see Elizabeth and you at the hospital."

"DI Turner collected us."

"Did she, now? Well I can't thank you enough for being here for us."

Janet took the trays to the kitchen and Hannah could hear her stacking the dishwasher.

"I think I'd better see you up to your room, before I go. God knows what the DI would do to me if I let anything else happen to you."

Slowly they made their way up the stairs. Janet stopped outside the bathroom. "I won't follow you in," she joked.

"I'm glad to hear it." Hannah thought about taking a shower but worried she might keel over so she just cleaned her teeth and removed what was left of her make-up.

After settling her in bed, Janet paused at the door. "Never a dull moment with you, is there?" She smiled but Hannah could read the fear in her face. "I'll be back early in the morning so don't worry about anything, okay?"

Hannah nodded. "Thank you." She snuggled down into her bed and reached for *Birdsong,* but she had nodded off before the door was closed and locked by Janet who then got into the car waiting to take her home.

* * *

Hannah woke and saw the radio alarm registered 03.44. What a strange time to wake up. She ached all over and her fingers were pounding with pain. The bedside lamp was still on and she reached for the analgesics the doctor had prescribed, left by Janet on her bedside table. Slowly she got up and went into Elizabeth's room. She was sleeping soundly.

Comforted, Hannah went back into her own room, turned off the lamp and went over to the window. Opening the curtains a fraction, she peered out into the street. The white van was still there. She wasn't sure if she should be reassured or more worried that something else might happen.

Back in bed she snuggled down as the painkillers began to take effect and she was able to go back to sleep. In her dream Tom was walking towards her saying, "I'll phone you soon..."

The ringing woke her. "Hannah – are you okay?" James' voice sounded distant.

"I'm fine. Just a bit bruised."

He said something she couldn't hear. "Sorry, I'll have to go. I'm due in theatre. I'll call you later."

There was a light tap on the door. Janet's head appeared. "I heard your voice and... oh, Hannah, what's happened?"

"Nothing. It's just..."

Janet sat on the side of the bed and held Hannah in her arms while she sobbed. She didn't move until they heard Elizabeth calling. Janet brought the child to her.

Then left them together. By the time she returned with a breakfast tray for Hannah, Elizabeth was playing boo and blowing raspberries at her mother.

"Come along young lady – breakfast." Elizabeth looked about to protest. Then smiled at her mother. "Bye bye."

Hannah looked at the breakfast Janet had prepared for her. Grapefruit juice, scrambled eggs on toast, coffee.

"Thank you, Janet, I don't think I can eat anything."

"You have to or no tablets. Try a little…"

"Oh, by the way –?"

Janet paused as she was leaving the room. "Yes?"

"Who were the flowers from?"

The story – the one Hannah had been working on for so long – was front page news. Claudia had held a press conference acknowledging Hannah's work in exposing the murders of Amalia Kumar, Nadia Chopra and Yamsin Sagar. Hannah had become the story once again. Fortunately there were no photos that could identify her.

CHAPTER FIFTY

"Do you feel up to some visitors?"

Hannah hadn't even heard the doorbell. "Who is it?"

Janet didn't have time to reply before Mr Singh burst into the room. "Mrs Weybridge it is your very good friend, my daughter Alesha." Hannah almost laughed at his expression of concern when he noticed her bruises. "My wife has sent you one of her most special curries to help you recover. Better than all that takeaway food…"

Alesha nudged him. Hannah noticed she was looking happy and relaxed. "Daddy!"

"And I would like to introduce you to my sister, Tania and her daughter, Surjit."

The older woman came forward and took Hannah's hand. "Thank you. Thank you." Then she was overcome by tears.

Alesha took it upon herself to explain as brother comforted sister. "Ms Weybridge, my aunt had sent Surjit into hiding as protection –" Surjit was nodding vigorously and smiling like she'd never stop.

"I told my mother I didn't want to go through with the arranged marriage but we were warned that there would be consequences if I refused. Mummy got me away and although the family threatened her she would not tell them where I was. My mother can be rather fierce."

As she said that the whole family laughed. "But," said Mr Singh, "you have exposed the villains. And for that we are most humbly grateful."

Hannah still hadn't got a word in edgeways. "When

you are recovered, Ms Weybridge," said Surjit's mother, "you must come to us for a proper celebration with the whole family."

"Thank you." The words seemed inadequate but what else could Hannah say? She felt exhausted by such exuberance.

"We will leave you in peace," Mr Singh concluded. "The food is in your kitchen."

Goodbyes over, they left, and Hannah sank back into the sofa cushions feeling shipwrecked.

CHAPTER FIFTY-ONE

The car pulled up outside the house. Hannah was ready to leave. Apart from the strapping on her left hand, she didn't look any the worse for wear after being attacked at the Kumars.

"You look very smart." Janet smiled her encouragement.

"Thank you." Hannah kissed Elizabeth and left.

A uniformed officer opened the car door for her. Hannah took a deep breath and got in.

Hannah willed herself to breathe normally as the plane taxied along the runway at RAF Northolt and came to a stop. Claudia was standing next to her in full dress uniform. Seven uniformed police officers marched to the undercarriage which opened. A coffin covered by the union flag and an officer's hat was manoeuvred out, then hoisted on to their shoulders with one officer leading the way. They marched the short distance to the waiting hearse. The coffin was placed inside. The men saluted and passed either side then joined the line which included the Commander of the Metropolitan Police.

Then another person came into focus. In full dress uniform with a walking stick to aid him. Tom Jordan. The man who she had feared dead was walking towards her... Claudia gave her a gentle push. She stumbled then found her momentum and walked towards him until she was in his arms; she clung to him, oblivious to the sound of clapping which erupted around them.

They drew apart and Tom took her arm as they

walked towards the awaiting dignitaries. The hearse, she noticed, had left. Claudia was beaming at them.

Hannah knew this moment would stay in her memory forever.

And then three shots rang out.

CHAPTER FIFTY-TWO

The private room that Lord Gyles had hired in the Savoy overlooked the Thames. In spite of everything that had happened there was a party atmosphere. That the proprietor of *The News* had managed to organise this at such short notice was a tribute to his influence and the diplomatic skills of his PA.

Georgina Henderson glided across the room towards Claudia Turner. She handed her a glass of champagne. "I love a woman in a uniform," she said as she introduced herself.

Claudia laughed. "Fortunately I'm not required to wear it too often." She sipped her drink. "I wasn't sure this would go ahead after what happened."

"Another front page scoop on our rivals? Always something to celebrate."

Joe and Phil had just arrived and soon after James put in an appearance.

Rory was beaming. He had arrived a little late, having put the finishing touches to the front page and leaving it in the hands of Terry Cornhill who would join them later when he'd put the first edition to bed.

There was the tinkling of a spoon on a glass. Lord Gyles smiled at the Maitre d'.

"Ladies and gentlemen, we are here to honour..."

Hannah didn't hear any more. She had moved away and was standing by the window, staring at the riverside view. The Thames looked murky and hostile. She felt an arm around her shoulder and turned towards Tom. He was there. Alive and smiling but looking tired.

"I had no idea I was still on their hit list. Thank God, MI5 were prepared."

When the shots had been fired they had both fallen to the ground. Hannah wasn't sure if Tom had been hit. But seconds later they were being escorted into the building and stayed there until the all clear was given.

"The explosion in the café wasn't a terrorist attack. It was retribution from a branch of the Mafia which had been involved in the trafficking racket in the US. That's what I had been investigating. I couldn't tell you anything for fear of putting you more at risk."

"I don't understand how that marksman managed to infiltrate a military airport and…"

"There will be a full enquiry. But it won't all be public. That assassination attempt had been set up just before the remaining Mafia had been rounded up in New York. He had not been deactivated. At least our security services were on the ball."

The sound of applause made them turn back into the room. Lord Gyles had apparently finished his speech.

The Metropolitan Police Commissioner walked over to them. "I have to leave now but I'll see you in a few weeks' time, Tom. The Home Office will want to discuss your next appointment."

"Yes sir. Thank you."

As the commissioner moved away, Tom looked at Hannah.

"Don't answer now, but how do you feel about leaving London?"

THE END

ACKNOWLEDGEMENTS

The writing of *Songs of Innocence* owes much to all those who have supported me with the previous two Hannah Weybridge thrillers, especially Matthew Smith and the Urbane team. It is a privilege to be published by such a dedicated publisher.

My family and close friends are fabulous at keeping me positive when the self-doubt that all writers seem to be afflicted by looms large. And it is, as always, a joy to celebrate with them when the finished article is on the bookshelves.

My thanks are also due to the network of book bloggers who have allowed me to feature in their Q&As and contribute guest posts. And everyone who tweets, reads and reviews – you are indispensable and much appreciated.

Once again, I am indebted to Dr Geoff Lockwood for help with medical facts and Christine Mayle who answered all my questions about schools. Any inaccuracies are mine alone. A special thank you to fellow author Lesley Lodge who read the manuscript before submission – and was complimentary.

And thank you, the reader, for investing your time in Hannah's world. I hope you have enjoyed the adventure as much as I have creating it.

For most of her working life in publishing, Anne has had a foot in both camps as a writer and an editor, moving from book publishing to magazines and then freelancing in both. Having edited both fiction and narrative non-fiction, Anne has also had short stories published in a variety of magazines including *Bella* and *Candis* and is the author of seven non-fiction books. Telling stories is Anne's first love and nearly all her short fiction as well as *Dancers in The Wind* and *Death's Silent Judgement* began with a real event followed by a 'what if ...' That is also the case with the two prize-winning 99Fiction. net stories: *Codewords* and *Eternal Love. Songs of Innocence* is her third thriller starring investigative journalist Hannah Weybridge.

HAVE YOU DISCOVERED THE OTHER HANNAH WEYBRIDGE THRILLERS?

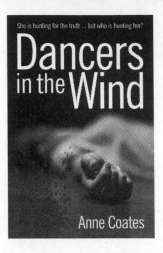

She is hunting for the truth, but who is hunting her?

Freelance journalist and single mother Hannah Weybridge is commissioned by a national newspaper to write an investigative article on the notorious red light district in Kings Cross. There she meets prostitute Princess, and police inspector in the vice squad, Tom Jordan. When Princess later arrives on her doorstep beaten up so badly she is barely recognisable, Hannah has to make some tough decisions and is drawn ever deeper into the world of deceit and violence.

Three sex workers are murdered, their deaths covered up in a media blackout, and Hannah herself is under threat. As she comes to realise that the taste for vice reaches into the higher echelons of the great and the good, Hannah understands she must do everything in her power to expose the truth ... and stay alive.

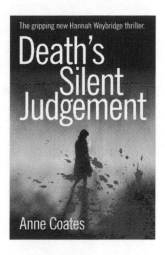

The gripping new Hannah Weybridge thriller.

Death's Silent Judgement

Anne Coates

DEATH'S SILENT JUDGEMENT is the thrilling sequel to *Dancers in the Wind*, and continues the gripping series starring London-based investigative journalist Hannah Weybridge.

Following the deadly events of *Dancers in the Wind*, freelance journalist and single mother Hannah Weybridge is thrown into the heart of a horrific murder investigation when a friend, Liz Rayman, is found with her throat slashed at her dental practice.

With few clues to the apparently motiveless crime Hannah throws herself into discovering the reason for her friend's brutal murder and is determined to unmask the killer. But before long Hannah's investigations place her in mortal danger, her hunt for the truth placing her in the path of a remorseless killer...

The series is very much in the best traditions of British women crime writers such as Lynda La Plante and Martina Cole.

Urbane Publications is dedicated to developing new author voices, and publishing fiction and non-fiction that challenges, thrills and fascinates.
From page-turning novels to innovative reference books, our goal is to publish what YOU want to read.

Find out more at
urbanepublications.com